ARMENDRICA

The Cult

Jay Laurent Merick

Cover created by The Raven Word

Published by Quartet Global Books 2025
First Edition

ISBN 978-0-9840493-2-5

Editor's Note

In this time of chaos, the author told me that In Armendrica
he found it impossible to write a standard novel. Why?
I asked him. His answer: Time in the Time of
Magatism isn't linear. It is not cyclical. In fact, in the
time of Magatism, there might not be any time at all
but a suspension of time. How can that be? Is it
possible to remove time from the sequence in which
events occur? Using the technique he calls the *flicker*,
Merick dissociates what we think of as "narrative
time" from the usual technique of linearity. But Merick
has also written this novel, as you will see, without the
"non-linear structure" that much of contemporary
writing tends to use to break the tedium of expectation
that has exhausted, as John Barth commented, the
modern novel.

The *flicker* can at any moment in this diversion Merick
calls a *novel,* drive us into a deceptive time. E.g. the
flicker can move us into the past or it can remain
static—that is to say, as Merick tells me, the *flicker* can
sit juxtaposed to a more traditional narrative moment
without breaking the time continuum.

So what is time in this novel, *Armendrica*? If Merick
rejects linear time, if he rejects non-linear narration,
what is left?

The question, Merick tells me, is not about time itself but
of time and the mind of the writer juxtaposed to time
and the mind of the reader. To help the puzzled
reader—and in the beginning, I was that reader—
Merick also told me he introduced a "measure" that
does move time—in some instances backwards or
forwards to events that precede a current narrative
"station" and that if the reader stacks those measures
into a non-authorial order, a linear narrative can—but
does not always—appear. Once the reader realizes that

there is, despite the author's assertions, both an implied linear time and an equally implied non-linear time in each "narrative event," the question of time is no longer a problem but is, in fact, a narrative technique called *late style*.

Merick, despite my insistences, states that *Armendrica* is not an experimental work nor is it a modernist tract and certainly not a member of the SMOF club.

In our discussions, Merick introduced me to the **You**. Note, he added, that the You is here capitalized just as other beings in this work are capitalized. I ask why. He told me that when Major Magat steered *Armendrica* into the Zaniistic-Skumic Abyss of Ignorance, Defeatism, Hopelessness, and Terror, every Armendrican—Blue, Red, Yellow, Green, Purple—is in part destroyed and the only way to make that clear is to reach out to You, the reader, to bring You, the healing reader, into Armendrica—You, the reader who dares to read *Armendrica*—and to show You how it feels to follow an entire nation into the horror of White Christian Thanatopia.

Merick rebelled when I first suggested that we include the **Glossary** as an end-piece rather than as footnotes but he later agreed that it is best if You, the Reader, have a roadmap to guide You on your travels through this perilous and dangerous tour of Magatistic treason and its disasters.

The Editor

Author's Note

Armendrica isn't another run-of-the-mill escapist-nazi-dystopian tract or a what-if novel of political retribution. I have written twenty-four books, but *Armendrica* is the first novel I knew I had to write, a novel that compelled me to write it. *Armendrica* is a novel that demands a new and distinctive style that departs from the Standard Model of Fiction. It is the novelist's job to join the resisters in the novel so that the novel itself becomes—by acts of defiance—a form of resistance.

He will skin you alive. All of you.
—Anon

Every act of Defiance is an act of Resistance.

Table of Contents

August. Year Three of the Culling

Armendrica is dismal this time of year. Gray skies. Rain. The concrete barricades divide the streets, the neighborhoods, the cities, the nation.

Left side. Right side.

And the blood.

Buckets of testicles splashed on the monuments in the Capitol. Left to dry for crows. The takers of souls.

And the skin.

Black skin. Brown skin. Yellow skin. On flag poles, curtain-thin skin, skin starred with fifty stars and scarred from razors. Pain long since silenced to an echo through the time of The Culling, the time of the Peelatorium and the Castratorium.

The banners and slogans still stand along the Magat-side streets—

White Choice, the Only Choice
MAGA
MAWA
Make Armendrica White Again
Down with Brown
Vermin Poison our Blood
I am White.
I am Christian.
Your rules don't apply to me.
Lock'em up
OK. OK.OK.
4/20
13/51
1488
J6
Day One

August 24th was first day in the first year of the Culling. The Magats hunted down the first Darkskins—Brownskins, Blackskins then the first Yellowskins. Only when the Captos found the money in death, did they come for the Whiteskins—the Progs, the Libtards—White was hard for Magats. Without uniforms and symbols and signs, civil wars make hard choices for the fighters. Who to kill, how to kill. No uniform? The killers looked for other signs. I refused to choose between the red hat and the blue hat. My sign was the Rainbow. By choice.

The cities in Armendrica now eat their dead. The Magats didn't know it, but the theocratic experiment failed on Day One and the result was Thanatopia—The death-world the Magats created on the only blue spot in the cosmos.

We knew it was coming, but we didn't know when.

Flicker—Weight room at Hawks training camp, first day of The Culling. Big Black , and Big White men working hard on the bars. The scent of sweat thick as blood.

October. First Year of the Culling

In October of the First Culling Year, I found two kids. Hiding in a Magat palace with its Hakenkreuze still glued to the walls. Against the background of the Schutzstaffel insignia hung a photo-portrait of the owner and four members of the Pride saluting Major Magat painted as a heroic savior in a ray of golden sunshine.

The street had switched sides—back and forth—Magat to Prog to Magat to Libtard to Anti.

Yaya and Yuyo had hidden until the Progs drove the last Magat out of the neighborhood.

Children can see me. Talk to me. Hear me. They have no shame. They have no guilt, but fear does eat them and fear robs them of their innocence. For them, there is now no casual walk in the sunshine. Armendrica cleft in two.

Yaya told me that she and Yuyo had eaten nothing for two days. Yaya told me she and Yuyo were afraid to go out during the killing because they knew that if one of the "Burlies,"—she called them "Burlies"—one of the Pride or the Minor Magats caught them they'd kill them and skin them because they were not white. MAWA.

Yaya was sixteen. Bright. Clean. Black hair. Epicanthic fold in the eyes. Her softness gone, as is the softness of all children when they have lost hope.

Yuyo—big for fourteen and hungry. Curious even in that time of purification—the first stage of Thanatopia—the racial cleansing of Armendrica, which meant the expulsion of any color but white.

Where is your mother?

Arrested.

And your father?

Flicker—a high rise in Laurentia looking over Lake Saint-Laurent.

A dejected Julia sits with her mother. On Julia's hands. Rough.

Long nails. On the Mother. An ancient face. A caring face.

We don't know. After his transition, she left us.
Where did she go?
I don't know.
Who took your mother, Yaya?
Magats. Big Magats. With guns. She made us hide. I'm hungry.
Where did they take her?
I think she's dead. Maybe our father…well. Yuyo says we have two mommies but now with Julia gone we don't have even one. Do you live here?

Flicker—A woman wearing gray prison pantaloons and jerkin. At a tribunal. She stands upright. Unbeaten. Undefeated. Rebellious. On the jerkin, in capital yellow letters

RACE TRAITOR

No. I don't have a home.
Everybody has a home.
Not everyone. Not now.
Where do you sleep?
I sleep where I fall down at night.
Why haven't the Magats killed you?
They would if they knew where I hide but Magats see only what they want to see, believe only what they want to believe.
Will you sleep here?
No. I want you to come with me.
Yuyo? Or just…me?

I'm not like that, Yaya.

I can't leave Yuyo. He'll die without me. He's hungry. I'm hungry. It's been a long time since we had even an apple.

You both come with me. I have fruit.

Are you going to kill us? And skin us?

I will never hurt you, Yaya. I can help you. Feed you.

I don't want to go with you.

You can't stay here. The Minor Magat might come back.

He won't come back.

How do you know he won't come back?

We saw them take him away.

Who took him, away?

I don't know.

Did they skin him? One of their own? The Magats?

I don't know.

Red caps?

No.

Blue caps?

No. What happened to your eye?

An accident in the China Sea.

You've seen the ocean?

And the mountains. And the deserts. And the jungles. I've seen the world. Come with me and I'll tell you stories.

Are they ugly stories? All stories now are ugly stories.

I'll tell you stories about sunset in the Andes, about sunrise in Tahiti and the coral reefs in Kukulkania and I'll tell you how young people before the Culling had dreams and hope and were kind to others.

Do you have kids?

No I don't.

Then how do you know what kids want?

I was a kid and I know this—I wanted to be happy. I wanted to be safe. I wanted to eat…

Pizza? Did they have pizza when you were a kid?

Pizza and ice cream and pumpkin pie.

I've never had pumpkin pie.

I know. No one can bake anymore.

And they don't have pizza anymore. Anywhere.

Come away from here with me and I'll bake you a pumpkin pie. Just for you and Yuyo. You can eat the whole pie.

He won't hardly eat anything after Mommy…went away. I think I better to stay here.

It's dangerous if you stay here.

I don't care.

May I hug you, Yaya? Things have changed so much now that there is almost no one you can trust and hug.

Just hug? Me? And Yuyo?

With me, you're safe. Always safe.

I look at Yuyo. He has fallen asleep on the sofa. He is peaceful, quiet, at rest. Yaya has nodded off, chin to her chest. Breathing shallow.

From the Minor Magat's cache, I draw two blankets. Armendrican Army blankets. Heavy. Thick. I cover each child and then I curl up on the floor to find my own peace.

But aware.

Always aware of the sounds and the shifting air. Aware of the buzz and hum and the threat. And then I fall asleep. In sleep, I dream—never good dreams of good things…Not now. Now that they have taken control of death.

Flicker—January. One Year Before the Culling. Exterior, the Great Hall of Magat Justice.

OPN

I watch her, DXM, standing outside the Great Hall. She knows what she is doing. She is neither large nor small, neither short nor stout. A graceful woman neither young nor old. Ageless skin. Graying hair—trimmed. Precise. Short.

She enters the Great Hall. She hears everything. She sees everything, remembers everything she sees and hears but she says nothing as she moves. Recording as she watches, as she listens in stealth-mode…the only way to survive now that MM Seashol has silenced the voices of journalists, branding us as traitors—for one reason only— we spoke and wrote truth about him and MM Seashol cannot tolerate truth…

DXM is like me and other Truth-tellers—invisible to those who won't see, won't hear, refuse to feel what is right in front of them. She hesitates as she scans the golden plaque on the wall. The plaque—the mantra, the slogan, the written law of the Magat White Christian Thanatopia borne out of the diseased mind of a diseased man and blessed with the diseased hands of the theocrats.

I am white. I am Christian.
Your rules don't apply to me.
I obey only the word of the Holy god.

Inside the Great Hall, nine Magat Justices sit around a circular table set with a feast of glazed squab, lemon asparagus, a spiral cut bone-in ham. Cut crystal wine goblets. Nine carafes, nine different wines, each placed in front of a MJ. Each cut crystal goblet hand-crafted in a unique style for each MJ. Gold utensils set along-side hand- painted Limoges China, each place setting unique.

The MJs, in their black robes, each robe a tight- wrapped shield that could be made of steel.

They eat in silence.

They drink in silence.

Servants—Blackskinned, tall, muscular, clean-shaven, bald, white-gloved, penguin-tailored knife-sharp creased tuxedos, black shiny shoes—stand behind each MJ's high-backed, gold leafed, hand-carved dining chair. The servants clear each plate as their MJ finishes—the squab.

Asparagus.

A slice of ham.

A glass of wine.

They then replace each wine goblet as their M.J. polishes off their wine. Then—fresh goblet, fresh wine. Clean hand-painted Limoges china plates.

The MJs lean back in their hand-carved, gold leafed dining chairs.

Silence.

The Chief MJ waves their hand, the Blackskinned servants all lean in as the Chief MJ says,

You boys may take the leftovers home. Coffee now.

The Blackskinned servants clear the dining table. In silence.

The Chief MJ waits until the servants are gone then they stand, belches.

You talked to them, Tommy. Do they know what they want?

MJ 1 : No one is sure what they want.

MJ 3: Then we have to give them everything.

MJ 4: Yes. Give them everything they want.

Chief MJ: Even if we don't know what they want?

MJ 5: The only way to satisfy Major Magat is to give them everything they want.

Chief MJ: But how can we give Major Magat everything they want if they don't know what they want?

MJ 6: Either give them everything they want, even if they don't know what it is they want, or you know what will happen and it won't be pretty.

MJ 7: Yes. Look at what they did to the Circuit Courts when they refused to give them what they want.

MJ 8: If we give them everything they want without knowing what they want, they will do what they want when they find out what they want and we won't know what they want until they do what they want and then where does that leave us?

Chief MJ: So we have no choice—give Major Magat everything they want even if they don't yet know what it is exactly that they want.

MJ 1: We might as well gut the Constitution if we give them everything they want before we know what they want.

MJ 2: Gut it? Yes. Gut that worthless, worn-out socialist piece of shit.

Chief MJ: Are you ready for that? Do we have any idea that's what they really want?

MJ 3: What they really want even after we give them everything they say they want but still aren't satisfied they will think there is something we haven't given them and that makes them turn vindictive.

MJ 4: They are after all a spoiled, narcissistic child with behavior problems, an enormous appetite for junk food and golf.

Chief MJ: The walls have ears, so be careful what you say.

MJ 2: I'm not sure we can give them everything they want, even…

Chief MJ: Yes, yes, if they don't know what they want how will they know that what we have given them is what they wanted?

MJ 5: Has anyone actually talked to Major Magat to find out what it is they want?

Chief MJ: I had a short talk with them but even after we parted I wasn't entirely sure of what it is they want, but I have a good idea that it will play hell with what they are calling that communist inspired piece of eighteenth-century bullshit.

MJ 4: Or blood. They do have a taste for blood.

MJ 2: We have to rewrite it anyway, so let's just give them what they want and let them figure out what we've given them and we will know then whether it's what they wanted. Or not.

MJ 4: Or not what?

MJ 5: So. It's decided? Give them what they want. No limits. No constraints?

Chief MJ: Absolutely. Unless you see another way.

MJ 4: Yes. No. Maybe. But this isn't an issue for the voters to go sticking their noses in and thinking they have a say in it because what we do is the law and that piece of trash might as well be…how did that Banjo guy say it? His word ain't worth the paper it's written on? They are the Major Magat and they have been given to us to guide us out of the libtard, prog-hell the socialist framers who wrote that constitution piece of shit have led us into.

MJ 3: Where is that coffee?

MJ 8: Those boys are probably lazing off drinking it in the kitchen.

MJ 2: Those boys ought to stick to sports.

MJ 1: Yeah. Those boys gotta learn to just shut up and dribble.

MJ 2: They do make good waiters, don't they?

MJ 4: That's all they're good for. Is there a way we can get rid of them?

MJ 2: All of them?

MJ 4: All of them.

Chief MJ: I know that that's one of the things Major Magat wants.

MJ 2: So, are you certain that there is something they want that they know they want?

Chief MJ: Oh yes. Absolutely certain about that.

MJ 4: How do you feel about that Tommy?

MJ 1: If they know that's what they want, then I'm in favor of giving them what they say they want and be finished with it.

MJ 4: I'm certain that if we give them what they want it will end in lots of blood.

MJ 1: Some blood?

MJ 4: More than some—gallons of blood.

MJ 2: What have those boys done with our coffee?

I walk with DXM out of the Great Hall. I see what she saw, smell what she smelled. The scent of blood and coffee thick in our nostrils. She has seen everything from the beginning of time.

She has birthed and seen birthed both abominations and redeemers. She has birthed and seen birthed both idiots and minds that understand the cosmos but she is not at fault that this time—the end of times—comes on the blade of a knife to the throat—this time of the Culling. And she has recorded what she has seen. It was she who wrote "To Dead Armendricans" in the earliest days to expose MM Seashol's tyrannical mind. But now, she has to, as do I, mask her truths, hide her words as we live in fear of the autocratic, theocratic liar, thief, chiseler and rapist who calls himself Major Magat Seashol.

This time, we have documentation. In detail. No guessing now about how or how many or when, in this time of killing and cutting and skinning…the Culling.

November. Three Years Before the Culling

It was a virulent cold day—not unusual for Sinverguenza—the day I entered the Office of Strategic Violence. They know me there—after the days, months, years I have spent mining them for my articles published…before MM 1…when the word "Truth" had not been stolen by the Magats and turned into a chant for chaos. Without Truth, there is no progress.

A cluster of Progs sat at a conference table, a map spread out.

There were eight of them—young, old, gray, black, brown, men, women, trans— The Prog Rainbow. Here, I feel at home. The Progs can see me, hear me, feel me, but I stand back observing, noting, thinking with them, without being with them. I write, I report, I don't make the news.

Leaning against a wall, I ease the ache in my leg, the pain in my shoulder. In the pain-dazed, semi-euphoria, I listen to the Prog colonel, her voice not the soporific, controlled voice of order and obey, but a voice full of command and commonsense. The kind of voice you want in a leader when you know you are going into battle.

The first thing that's clear from this map is that we won't fight the future Armendrican civil war with invaders at our borders but with our next-door neighbors because we're all mixed together…

Colonel, it hasn't gotten that bad yet.

It will. When Major Magat gives the word, there will be fire. Again.

We control the Army.

We do not control the Army, Captain. We control that part of the Army the Magats have not infiltrated. Our recruiters are on the ball, but enlistments are down…

But we do control ammo production and

distribution.

When Major Magat steps in, we'll have that fight on
our hands, too.

Loyalty?

*Forget Loyalty... to anything. Think Fealty. Think a
return to a medieval liege-vassal relationship, Captain, but
let me continue— We do not have a North/South or
East/West Divide. We have an intra-urban/rural divide.
And this means that most Armendricans, in most cities, live
near or around others who disagree with them and they
resent those who disagree with them and the political truth
is that there is no cohesion in the country. Polarized
disagreement has created a divide that can't be bridged
except with blood. And that means Armendrican blood.*

You are sure of this, Colonel?

*Our deep sources tell us that the Technoautocratic
threat escalates with each rally MM holds and the more
favorable coverage he gets. But back to the map. While we
tend to think of cities as these huge integrated urban hives,
even liberal Verguenza has its share of red dots. ...*

Which means?

*Which means that women are the key and the key is
red because white male privilege with its gun-madness
benefits any woman who doesn't want to give up her
privileged position.*

Where do we have any advantage then?

*We have history. We have science. The Magats
don't read now. They see science as a corruption of their
holy god's plan. No Magat understands anything but the
bullet in their AR 15.*

How do we proceed from here, Colonel?

*We wait. We prepare. We train. This war will be
bloody, Captain.*

*Flicker—A barricaded street in Armendrica City.
Fires burn. Cars burn. Headless bodies smolder. The*

The pain in my leg shoots up and into my back. The pain wipes me out. I settle into a brain fog that controls me. I go blank. Call it what you like—PTSD, shell shock, battle fatigue—you get it when you fight and the people you fight are hard and real and know how to sling bullets at you.

Sometime later, I find a way out of the pain the way you find your way out of a bad dream—shaking, angry that in this time the pustule of hate is growing and festering and in the pustule there is the killing and the killing will erupt because Major Magat has dreams of retribution and prison for anyone who opposes him—that means did not vote for him—and punishment just the way all his fascist predecessors ordered it and the blood they spill is never their own. History repeats itself as if being alive demands and expects the needless killing—stupid in an Age of Dreams that there should be terror, and fear and tyranny and the Culling…always the Culling the Darkskins….

Without glancing at the map—I know it so well, have seen it before, have seen the red dots that will flame up with death and destruction, the kind of destruction that the Bear brought down on his dissidents in their cities with his violent reclaim of long-dead empires.

I exit the Office of Strategic Violence. Pain so intense it blurs my mind, the stiffness in my shoulder a reminder of what I left behind last time I dropped from a helo in the Occupied Zones to cover the wars of annexation, to map out the burial grounds, to write about the fear and death I saw. And for what?

*Flicker—Eight bearded, burly, bulky Magats in
camo gear. AR 15s. Riding the bed of a pickup. Decals on
the pickup—MAWA. 1488. Day One*

August 24th Day One of the Culling

Magatism exploded the day the Magats raided the Hawks. Magats. They entered at dusk, after practice, smashed into the weight room where the Hawks sweated at the weight bench. Big, beefy men with angry eyes from time spent in the trenches working for their Capto owners—white men in tailor-made silk suits, rich white men who bought and sold and traded human meat.

Magats.

Kicking in the doors, the eight Minor Magats with 15s, cut loose, freezing the Hawks. Shouting, down on your knees, boys and don't do nothin' stupid 'cause we don't want holes in that skin.

The Hawks knelt and two Magats zip-tied hands behind backs.

Three White Hawks rose—a defensive wall of bodies, but a Magat raked the ceiling with a burst from his AR 15 told them to stand still or die.

And they stood.

Did nothing.

And the Magats herded six Black Hawks out of the training room into a white van with MAWA stenciled on the side.

And when the Magats and their captives disappeared, the White Hawks—confused, crushed—did not return to their sweat routines.

I watched—as I always watch—not commenting, not interfering, taking notes, recording it all so that when the time comes, there will be evidence. Not alternative facts, but evidence. Visual. Auditory. All recorded.

The van headed down Verguenza, away from Hawk Stadium, to the freeway…

Flicker—Castro meat Packing Sector. Interior of a castratorium. Six black players. Huge men. Hanging by their heels. Castrated. Peeled.

Flicker—Six human skins hooked to the handrail of the I-5 overpass at Madison Street. A sign dangles from each skin.

MAWA.

I see myself for what I am— a catalog of the past, an oracle speaking the future, a clockwork god in Voltaire's clockwork universe.

I can do nothing once the Magats start the machinery of death that leads to their Thanatopia…I recall reading about death and resurrection and how the ancients believed that if you shoved enough bodies into the underworld, some of them would, in time, return—physical resurrection. Thanatopia. The City of Death.

February. One Year Before the Culling

Flicker—A fortified warehouse in the Sinverguenza Central District. Progs in control of confiscated ammunition production. Hundreds of cases of arms and ammunition. 9 MM. 7.5 FK. M 240. RPGs. Tons of steel. The tools of death. Equipment. Ammo belts. Comm units.

Flicker—Speaker at the Seawenn Conference on the Final Solution to Democracy stands at a conference table. Projected on the wall a list—
    Date—August 24.
    Time—9:00 PM
    First Target—Hawks
    Process—Capture. Castratorium. Peelatorium.
    Location of Public Display of Hides—Freeway Overpass
    Thirty days after first capture initiate Leather Exports Prerugginian vehicle industry.

OPN

August 25th Day Two of the Culling

I enter the tabernacle
It's a splashy, gilded tabernacle with a golden pipe organ
I see Magats in MAWA caps
 Rows of red caps
The preacher shouts that the Holy God is punishing all those satan lovers
Taking their hides
Just what does LGBTQA mean
It means sin and lust and fornication and confusion with men cut as women mating with women cut as men and all of them spitting on the Holy God who made the human and they will pay the price for denying the Holy God when the rapture comes while we the believers…
We… will… all… be… transported….
just like that…
snap of his fingers
And the Holy God will wipe all the satanists from the earth and start again Yes Start again, and the world will be white again
All white again
I watch the preacher crucify a naked pre-op trans Darkskinned man.
Is he dead?
Drugged?
Is he an Immie?
Kukulkanian?
Kleisthenesian?
Prerugginian?
Then, armed with a scimitar flaying knife the preacher skins the trans and as he peels the skin from the body there is blood and as the skin falls away the

congregation chants

Make Armendrica White Again

Magattes swoon.
Drooling Magat men approach the offered body
each one dips a finger in the blood of the dead crucified
skinned trans and licks the finger

I limp out of the tabernacle
out into the sun
feel the heat
smell the fresh scent of flowers eating at the anger
in my nostrils.
Walking past the row of gilded limousines each
with its MAWA decal.
I still taste the blood of the man on the cross
I look at my right hand then at the left
—no index finger, no thumb. Parts of me left in the
sand and grit and wind from the wars in the Occupied
Zones and the search for Truth. Truth. Now, as others have
written—in war, Truth is the first casualty.

July. Five Years before the Culling

Flicker—The desert, a wrecked Humvee on its side. A soldier holds his left wrist, a wrist with no hand. He looks up into an endless sky. Blood on his face. A shoulder patch on his right sleeve—the flag of Armendrica. Second Airborne Battalion. Special Ops.

Flicker—The Magat Preacher sodomizing a twelve-year-old Blackskin boy. A Magatte watches. She sits in a red velvet chair. Her dress bunched up around her waist. She masturbates with a leather-bound Major-Magat-autographed bible until she orgasms.

Flicker—The Conference on the Final Solution to Democracy. Around a table, a dozen white men wearing silk suits, polished shoes. Hair clipped neat. On a large wall screen a map of Armendrica—the major cities from border to border coded red, blue.

DXM

July. Two Weeks Before the Culling

I go to a conference of Magat-money-men.
The hall is full.
I smell their cologne.
I hear the chatter.
Watch the hands on the tables.
The scent of money.

At a table with two Magats in silk suits, I listen to their chatter, their voices, raspy, breathy as though they have poisoned the air with their talk of money and women and the Blacks who don't know their place.

They do not see my scars. They do not hear my voice—a voice tainted by the gas and the sand in the wind of the wars in the Occupied Zones. I could tell them about the taste of ball powder propellant and how it burns the lungs. I could tell them about the cost of death and blood, but they already know everything and I am invisible.

Millions like me—men, women—invisible.

My wounds invisible, my lungs invisible, my sleepless pain invisible. Invisible my endless blood-dreams of armless, faceless, legless men lying in sand, dying on rocks, drowned in salt-water.

The Armendrican flag sewn to each of us.

They do not see, these Magats, in their silk suits and three thousand dhaler hand-made-in-the-Occupied Zones shoes, the wreck of men, the wreckage of women.

They hate wrecked-men, men who surrendered their bodies for a greater good. *Anti-Armendrican Progs they call the dead, the unachieved....*

Magats don't see men and women who have sacrificed their bodies and minds. They see only failed men and women who have failed to find gold, failed to become rich, failed to be the obese scum-sucking hyena-man living off the fat of his crimes.

A Plut. So many Pluts. So many crimes.

The speaker at the podium draws applause, so much applause he has to pause at the end of each utterance—

Welcome to the end of democracy.

(applause, cheers.)

We are here to overthrow it completely.

(heavy applause)

We didn't get all the way there on J 6

(wild cheers, hoots and applause)

but this time we will get rid of it and replace it with this… right…here.

In one hand he holds up a white cross on a gold necklace. In the other hand P 2025.

(shouts, cheers, applause, table-pounding cacophony)

After we burn the whorehouse on the river, after we gut the prog-men and send the prog-women back to the kitchen where they belong and after we impale and gut the traitors and the sex-traitors we will establish the new Armendrican Republic on its ashes.

(**Make Armendrica White Again**.)

Our first order of business will be righteous retribution for those who betrayed Major Magat and by betraying Major Magat betrayed Armendrica and betrayed the Holy God who made us Great.

(**Make Armendrica Great Again**.)

And now, the moment you have been waiting for. Get out your checkbooks and write, write, write because we want to—

(**Make Armendrica Great Again**.)

Major Magat strolls out of the wings of the conference room. He carries a foot-long gold cross in his right hand. He wears a ten-inch gold cross on a chain around his neck.

(**Make Armendrica Great Again**.)

He holds up the cross to a roomful of silence.

Religion. Religion is such a great thing it's so it keeps you know there's something to be good about you want to be good you wanna it's so important I don't know if it's explained right I don't know if I'm explaining it right you know you wanna be good you wanna go to heaven when you have something like that you wanna go to heaven OK so you wanna go to heaven so if we don't have heaven OK you almost say that's the reason why I do have to be good let's not be good what difference does it make so write those checks and you know why you love the Holy God?

(Make Armendrica White Again.)
(Make Armendrica Great Again.)
(Make Armendrica White Again.)
(Make Armendrica Great Again.)

Flicker—In a Magat palace, on a wall, the standard portrait of Major Magat as God, Jesus Christ, and Hitler rolled into one—complete with radiant cape, fur collar, shining white armor, gold sneakers and on the opposite wall, a portrait of Major Magat holding a bible. Naked except for the cape and his MAWA cap he is raping a chain-bound and gagged black woman.

DXM

May. Ten Years Before the Culling

I first met OPN after his tour of the Occupied Zone. He looked older than I expected. Taller than I expected. From the corner of Oliveira Boulevard and Canyon Street. I watched him, already a legend to everyone in the Armendrican Press for his coverage of the Sand Wars. He wore a green campaign cap and in the sunlight the badges glistened. A green uniform—not an official Armendrican Army uniform but with a hint of the same. Thick, black, long hair down to the shoulders of his green jacket. Neglect in the locks? No. No brush had touched that head in a long time. I remembered the photos he published with his articles but the man I saw was not that younger man. His beard now trailed down to his chest. A thick, black, full beard. Yet there was no connection there between the black hair and the beard and the gait of the man. I noticed the locked left knee. The left boot scraped the pavement as he walked and I recalled a story about his wound and how, wounded, he had lain in the sand and the heat but came back to write about tyranny and death.

A man's feet are his foundation and when the foundation is cracked, broken, in danger, is the man himself on the verge of destruction? Was he on the verge? Listening to him that day in the interview with a scholar who had studied Timothy and the history of tyranny my only question was why was he there? In this city? In Armendrica when he had connections everywhere in the world?

I asked him later how he knew the storm was gathering and he said that the seeds are dhalers and when the dhalers grow to billions there is no wall that can withstand the storm. He said that he had witnessed the clouds in Teutonknia and he predicted it for Armendrica.

He predicted the Technoautocracy. He predicted AMM2

In that interview, that day—I listened to OPN work. I admired his skills as he grilled the author's foundation—

"What is a criminal and a Criminal Code when the criminals control everything from the top?"

"Tyranny."

"What is corruption when the entire chain of command is corrupt?"

"Tyranny."

"What is it when fortunes become political?"

"Tyranny of the moneyed class. But you know that."

"What is it when the rich crook becomes a doctor becomes a lawyer becomes a politician?"

"Tyranny. You have read Timothy. You know that. When men see money and privilege as pointers to power, they show that they can buy everything and everything can be bought and once bought controlled and for them law has no meaning because their money allows them to buy the law and with that they buy the death of democracy."

"What do you see coming?"

"Tyranny, of course. It's a matter of time."

"Matter of time?"

"Let me put it this way—Tyranny comes in inverse ratio to the education level of the electorate and Armendrica is dropping into an abyss of ignorance. Erase education and you speed up the speed of ignorance. It is a matter of time now."

August 25th Year One of the Culling

The crowd of deplorables in the amphitheater is monstrous, enormous, noisy, belligerent and the raucous insults grow louder when Major Magat steps out of the wings to the podium.

He wears a clown suit. His hair a bright orange curly tangle flares up and over his head as if it were a balloon trying to lift him up.

His hat is an outsized fedora with two hog ears sprouting from either side—hog ears the size of ham slices.

The skin of his face is dyed death-mask charcoal gray.

His huge lips flap as he waddles to the podium giving him the demeanor of a large orange hungry duck on its way to the trough.

Three shades of red polka dots splash over his carrot-colored shirt, a shirt held in place with massive red suspenders.

His pants—flared from waist to ankles—bulge and wriggle as if a small herd of pigs has gathered at his crotch in search of dinner.

His size 25 shoes—laced up to his ankles with bright red strings— slap the floor as he walks to the rhythm of his deplorables chanting—

Make Armendrica White Again
Make Armendrica Great Again

He raises both hands—huge white gloves, bulging sausage-shaped fingers—and gives an awkward middle finger salute to the Armendrican flag posted to his right.

The deplorable cluster of sycophants howls in unison—

Make Armendrica Great Again
Make Armendrica White Again
Lock'em Up. Lock'em Up
Gut the Libtards
Skin the Blackies

Hands up, he speaks, but the deplorables' chant grows louder and as Major Magat's lips flap, the words tumble out as though coming from a random-word generator.

We can't undo what's done because we are the greatest I am the greatest president Armendrica possible anywhere in the universe and I am the Perfect One and we are here to celebrate me and only me 'cause a tall woman told me that she was going to vote and she did and all the pretty women love to get their pussies grabbed like doughnuts and that's where we are gonna go when we deport ten million of the infected vermin immie rapists and murderers and drug addicts who are stealing your jobs just like the libtards stole my election and that's the word of the holy god who made strawberries and peaches and fish and everything we eat comes from the holy god and I am the god born to lead you to the next time you don't have to vote 'cause we've got it, yes we have got purge and clean and make Armendrica White Again and we are gonna make Armendrica white again and what it takes is make'em do it with gun in their face.

And the deplorables erupt and somewhere there is gunfire and the chant escalates into a random cacophonic word salad….

Make Lock'em up Darky Intruders death kill libtards make

Armendrica pure great holy god kill everything that wears

Blue make Armendrica pure and white and great

white choice only choice women on their knees
your body my choice and in the kitchen kuche
Kirke jesus son mother fucker….

I follow Major Magat off the podium, follow him
and his coterie of advisors and sycophantic Technos and
murderers and planners and as I follow the Perfect One and
his entourage to the limos waiting in the bowels of the
auditorium I see the vulturine Pluts clapping Major Magat
on the back and showering him with packets of hundred
dhaler bills and oil shares and toilet paper and silk and gold
threaded cloth and they are the same Pluts I watched at the
Seawenn Conference the day they laid out their plan for the
deporting and extermination of the Darkskinned people
who, the Pluts said, did not belong in a White Armendrica.
A photographer snaps shots of the Perfect One in his clown
suit as he grabs a woman's pussy and kisses at her, his
yellowish duck-bill lips flapping before he slides into a
black limo that oozes out of the garage and into the dismal
gray day that is the color of Major Magat's charcoal gray
face.
		In the air, I still hear the chanting—Great Again.
White Again. Deport'em. Kill'em. Holy God.
		The Minor Magats are on the loose.
		No restraints now.
		No stopping them now.
		I exit, smell the putrid air, feel the noxious fumes of
the residue of ugliness invade my lungs.
		I am sickened. A sickness unto dying.
		I am hurt. My leg hurts. My shoulder nags its slow
persistent pain. Fought for. So many died …there…in the
Occupied Zones so the Minor Magats can hate. Kill and
maim and destroy without fear of justice.
		I knew this is the end…but…but…but…

DXM

July. Six Months Before the Culling

The weight of corruption was smothering Armendrica.

I felt it.

I tasted it.

I smelled it.

Corruption.

OPN and I had tracked it in the Time Before the Culling and the deeper we dug into the cycle, the more potent the stench became, the heavier the weight became until the putrescence turned into a strangling miasma.

In the first days of the first cycle, the Cycle of the Contesting, I went to the Lake, to the Magat Palace and I waited. I don't hover, no need to conceal myself, because I am a woman and I am invisible to the gaze of these men.

I don't exist, have never existed except for the rare moments when they, in their Male Perfection, force my legs apart and enter me with their roughness to squirt their god-fluids into me before leaving me alone in the dark.

On my back or on my knees, I am every woman, at every minute of every life all women have lived and every woman is me living in the fear of the dark street, fearing a walk alone in a night-time of rape and murder and mutilation, afraid, sitting in a dark corner in a dark house waiting for the knife, the gun, the clenched fist—and always, always dreading, dreading…the daylight….

I see them.

I remember them.

I have watched the millions of women torn and bloody, crying, prostrate in their submission, helpless to avenge themselves because the Justices weigh as much as the gelt that bought them weighs.

And at the Palace, I wait. I wait and I watch.

They arrive in limousines. Six of them. Suits of silk and silken shirts and they look like men who know what they are and what they are going to do. I follow them to the Magat Palace with its palm trees and clipped grass.

They leave their limos—six limos, six chauffeurs, twelve bodyguards armed with Uzis—in the driveway, parked side by side—no first here in a team of firsts.

These men are not the sewer rats who sell drugs to kids on their way home from school.

These are not the Minor Magats who believe everything the vulpine hate monger Media Master Magats throw at them.

These are the owners of men and women who do not know they are owned. These are men who do not light their own cigars or pour their own wine.

These are men who do nothing but who order everything done and what they order the Master Magat and Minor Magat do.

They do not have to account to anyone for anything because they are privileged, they are above, they are beyond—

The Law.

The Church.

Convention.

Beyond everything.

Servants. Young Black women, skin bare, bow to them as the men pass through the portico, walking on the red carpet, silk suits shining in the southern sun, shining the way armor always shines.

These are men who never get their shoes dirty. Do not get their hands dirty. Filthy men who live lives so filthy they reek as they breathe although no one ever tells them they stink.

I follow the wake of their scent into the Palace on the Lake.

In an enormous, gold-plated library—not a single

book—Major Magat sits in a gold-plated armchair—
padded with red velvet—that rests on a gold carpet with
gold dhaler signs woven into it.

A there is an odor.

I try to place the odor—it isn't any spice that I
know, no chemical smell that I know. It is an unwashed,
unclean, impure, rotten odor. I watch the men approach.
Major Magat stands and with the deference of a vassal to a
lord—he bows.

In the golden light flowing over the room, I see the
faint flicker of green, then gold, then silver then paper and I
watch the green fall off the men and Major Magat struggles
to his knees and gathers the green into his tiny fingers and
at that second I understand that it is the corrupt odor of
lucre in all its forms and the odor spreads over the men and
over Major Magat.

The odor is the effluence of some suppurating
fungal growth, the fungus of greed and self-love and hatred
of anything and everything that does not reduce to a
number in a numbered account—without a numbered
account there is no way to track the disease—and as the
men stand over Major Magat, I watch him gather the green
and the gold and the silver and the paper and stuff it into
his coat pockets and his pants pockets and when he has
gorged himself he racks back into his gold armchair and he
vomits.

The splurge of green and gold and silver and paper
that reeked of rot now reeks also of acid and death. The
skin of Major Magat's puffy face stretches. And he speaks,
his words garbled into a language no one has heard
before—the jargon of greed and filth and lust and rutting
and he mumbles,

You what? Get? Now?

And one of the men, the one with the strongest
scent of greed on him—it's as if he has a G tattooed onto
his forehead—grins and he says,

Everything, coast to coast, that the progs don't have nailed down.

No oversight, the second in command says.

No watchdogs, the third man says.

Free rein, the fourth man says. We run it, you do what we say.

No taxes on anything, the fifth man says.

No Parlezment interference, no committees, no investigations, the sixth man says.

Major Magat, retching green and gold and silver and patting the paper stacked on his swollen belly nods and he groans and he smiles and his teeth glisten a light shade of rot and he says,

Done.

The six men then turn, leaving Major Magat in his golden armchair, his chest heaving with the burden of corrupt breath. He stands. He wobbles as he stands. His belly tugs him to his knees and he rolls on his flab as if it is an exercise ball and he screeches,

What about Medved?

The men, all six of them, ignore him.

What about Medved? I gotta work it out with Medved.

The tall man laughs.

Fuck Medved, he says.

They leave the Palace.

Leave in their limousines with their bodyguards and their golden aura and their stench and rot and putrescence streaming out behind them—plumes of corruption fouling the air of Armendrica that all of us have to breathe.

I understand then that I have witnessed Major Magat selling a country to the Pluts.

I see OPN nod. He understands too. He has been on the trigger end of an M240. He has seen and written about the blood of empire mixed in the sands of death while the moneymen smoke their cigars and sniff their cocaine and murder and rape and with the flick of an ash from a cigar retire to their castles.

We know these men in limousines stand apart— invisible but for their stench—men who buy anything and everything without ever having to answer for their mistakes.

CPN and I are so much alike. Our wounds are the wounds of millions.

He says, Will you survive?

I will survive, but I don't know about Armendrica.

Flicker—Exterior of a hospital. A single ambulance. EMTs pull a Black woman from the ambulance. She lies on a gurney. She is naked. She is unconscious.

DXM

December. Fourth Month of the Culling

I am with Major Magat in the green room next door to the pressroom where the reporters wait. I feel the tension, smell the odor of Major Magat, hear the murmuring of the media testing and tasting the air, waiting for a sign of blood or the scent of death—which in the first months of the Culling has not been rare as the Minor Magats, after their first taking of the Black Hawks, have shown their intentions, intentions set down in the Seawenn Protocol, intentions now policy carried out across Armendrica with the dictated results—the annihilation of all Darkskinned vermin living in the cities, crossing the borders. Annihilation no matter how long their blood has been Armendrican—starting in Sinverguenza and working through Orgullo—and the press, the media—what remains of it—have reported nothing but what the Master Magats dictate.

In the greenroom, I watch Major Magat admire himself in the full-length mirrors that he now demands be there for every appearance.

He wears a dark blue suit. He wears a crisp white shirt. He wears a bright yellow tie knotted.

And he wears a red Stetson hat with a red hatband around the brim and in the hatband, there is a ring of crow feathers—bleached and dyed red to match the red caps members of the press wear as their own signs of submission and cowardly worship of this, the living god, the image of the Holy God who sees himself as the Perfect One.

Today, the Perfect One, Major Magat, wears shiny black leather gloves.

In his right hand he holds a bottle—I can't make out the label, but I know what's in that bottle.

He leaves the greenroom and strolls into the

pressroom to the complete silence of bootlickers and scum
suckers whose silence helped enthrone the Perfect One in
the early days—even knowing then what P 2025 meant but
failing to report one word of its cruel and deadly policy
measures infused with the stench of Lord Caryan's death-
wish.

The media members all rise, doff their red caps and
bow in deep homage—a profound submission to the Perfect
One with his orange hair implants and his bronzed skin that
glistens like gold in the pressroom light bulbs installed just
for the Perfect One so he shines as though cast in metal for
eternity—from the waist until their noses scrape the floor
and their butts—men, women, other—poke up oiled and
ready for the prong of The Perfect One if and when he
demands it. And he will demand it and they will yield their
asses to his cock as readily as they have yielded their minds
to his lies.

He stands at the dais. He sets the Bottle on the
podium. He speaks—This is a wonderful Armendrican
product made in Armendrica, a superior product that we
have many such good products tells us that we are the best
at making good products anywhere there are products such
as this and I have many products, products produced just
for you, I have books, books with my name on them and
shoes, shoes everyone wants to have because when you get
sick this is what you want and sometimes when you need a
wonderful product like this you also want and need meat
ready to eat to save the little woman the trouble of having
to go out and breathe the same air that the progs and lefties
and libtards breathe so your children, may the Holy God
watch out for them and get the fluoride out of their water
and give them the right meat they want and need when they
need and no vaccines, no vaccines in the water and want
meat that comes in cans and you will see the Truth on my
social network which is the best network there has ever
been and I am the finest and purest and smartest leader the

world has ever seen and that includes our friends Adolf and Mr. Lecter who is perfect after me because this is the new Armendrica and now canned meat the second most lucrative export and I ask and answer all my questions so you don't have to pay any attention or do anything except smile and sit there all pretty.

The Perfect One holds up the bottle. Waves it. A magic wand in the hand of a lunatic. Each member of the press writes on tablet. I walk through the crowd catching sight of what they write and I see that they have all written the same words—MM holds up a bottle.

At the podium, Major Magat, The Perfect One who looks like Jesus Christ, Hitler, and a Shining Knight in splendid gold armor, speaks and points at a press member but his finger wags and it's impossible to tell which reporter he wants but he commands—You come here and be blessed.

The murmuring in the press ranks exudes aws and ahs and ohs and oohs and the reporter who has never reported anything but what one of the Master Magats told him to report, walks with measured paces to the dais, mounts the dais and stands beside the Perfect One, eyes wide and then he gags.

He bends over and retches.

I see him swallow his vomit then with puppy dog admiration in his eyes, he smiles and the Perfect One holds up the bottle and on the bottle I see the words—

Major Magat's Herpetological Cure-All

At the back of the dais, a curtain opens and out of the wings two clowns whirl onto the stage, one doing back flips, the other doing cartwheels until they disappear then the curtain opens and two white women wearing white nurses' uniform and six inch heels trot onto the dais and as they trot they unfurl a banner with bright bold red lettering on it—

Major Magat's Herpetological Cure-All

Rub it on, rub one off, flush all your ills away.
Reborn in the new Armendrica.
From the wings a white man in a white doctor's
coat springs onto the dais. He holds a gigantic fake paper
hypo with the words FUCK SCIYINS
HYDOROROCHLROQUEENINE KILLS KOVID DED.
The fake doctor pretends to jab the retching reporter
with the fake hypo and then he disappears and the white
fake Magatte nurses in their white fake Magatte nurses'
uniforms fade back into the wings.
Major Magat elevates the bottle.
The reporter on his knees looks up with adoration
on his face, complete submission to the Perfect One in his
eyes. Major Magat, the Perfect One, the Perfect One says,
Open the bottle and you will be saved.
The reporter tries to open the bottle.
But there's nothing in the bottle.
Nothing? My Wisdom is nothing?
No liquid in the bottle, Perfect One.
Did I say my Wisdom was a liquid?
No, but…people think…
Just open the bottle and rub it on your skin.
The reporter twists the cap of the bottle and, holding
the lid in one hand, the bottle in the other, raises it. A
noxious odor, a stream of gray, miasmic fogginess. The
reporter sniffs the miasma and stands upright.
There. You see? You are cured. You are healed. I
am the Holy God brought to Armendrica to make
Armendrica White Again and people think what I want
them to think and they do what I want them to do and they
don't question me—the bottle empty? I could gun you
down right here and be standing with the gun in my hand

and I would tell them that you committed suicide and they'd believe me. You're so stupid. You're as stupid as the stupidest libtard.

But Oh Perfect One…I wasn't sick.

You puked, you little leftie reporter puke, you puked and puked…

The smell, Perfect One…the smell…of…your…farts made me puke…

Get this puke off my stage, in the name of the Holy God and throw him in one of the immie pits or in prison…

Four burly bearded Minor Magats appear on the dais and wrestle the reporter to the floor and drag him off by the heels and Major Magat turns to the assembly of wordsmiths in exile from truth and he points. He says,

Who's next?

I take a deep breath. The odor of Major Magat's body made the reporter puke. All I smell is the residue of what once was truth and knowledge but which now has changed into a gaseous cloud of hatred, confusion, distortion and….weirdery.

And out there, in Armendrica, the Culling goes on but no reporter writes about it. The skinning goes on but there is no journalistic outcry. The chaining and the whipping goes on while the press corps sit on their hands waiting for the next words of wisdom from the Perfect One who is leading them into the hellish bowels of oblivion in the dark city, to Thanatopia—eyes wide open.

DXM

August 24th Day One of the Culling

They cut the electricity at three A.M. The darkest moment of the night. The time of dying and pain. The time of self-death. Midnight in Thanatopia.

Armendrica City goes dark. Armendrica goes dark. And then, in the darkness, the sound of gunfire.

For hours.

I stand on the slope of Beacon Hill in the park with a view of Sinverguenza and the Sound. Across the Sound, I see Verguenza—the Sister City, once the city of light and kindness, the hub of art and writing, the mind-built center of the renaissance and the rise of critical thinking but there, too, in the dark, I see muzzle flashes dotting the darkness—unnatural sparks—and I know this is the tyranny of death.

Thanatopia.

At Seawenn, I watched the Magats lay out the plans for Thanatopia—the time-scheme, the areas of the cities showing first strikes—and I know that more Blackskins are headed for a peelatorium in the Malcriado District to be cut and skinned and butchered.

The first to die.

From the hillside, I trek down into the Culling and I see, in the darkness, in the light of flashlights raking bodies that there are hundreds of dead.

Torn.

Chopped.

Shot. Face. Neck. Head. Shoulder. Heart.

So many bodies—all wearing the blue cap or the rainbow cap.

Scattered among the blue caps, a few red caps.

And there are no weapons on the ground beside the dead.

It is clear to me as I stand over them, that this attack

was a surprise even though Major Magat had declared he would 'take back Armendrica from Day One and make it White Again.' We knew. I knew. He told us what he would do.

August. Day Six of the Culling

You walk on through the city—now a killing field. The smell of blood sharp in the air. The dark streets silent except for the rattling of gunfire. It is curious, the silence under the gunpowder thunder—no shouting, no pleading, no begging for mercy.

To either side of You, in front of You, behind You, the killing goes on. Muzzle flashes cascade in the falling for fireworks, the sound ricocheting through the darkness. Against the crack of ARs and the bursts of handgun fire, You hear the rapid-firing of heavy machine guns and the mechanical rumble of vehicles and You cannot imagine either the targets or the reasoning that put the killing machines in the streets of Sinverguenza but You know, from Seawenn, the why.

The dark city, house after house—silence and darkness and in the Leschi Neighborhood You walk around bodies riddled, still bleeding—men, women, children. You stop to touch the corpses of the young—cooling now, blood-slick now and then, against the white side of a house, You see movement. You stop. Kneel. Fear pounds in your chest, an unwelcome guest, but this is what Armendricans now live with—fear. Dread. Darkness.

You hear a door open, footsteps on the wooden porch of the house. Then silence.

You wait.

The killing grows louder in the darkness—but again, curious, there's no wail of sirens, no ambulances, no howl of helicopters descending—nothing but gunfire.

You creep closer to the house. You see the image of the snake on the flag and the words

Don't Tread On Me

A Magat house.

The house is unscathed.

No bullet holes.

No grenade blasts.

No glass broken.

You mount the wooden porch steps.

Outside, nothing. But You are sure You saw a figure in the dark in the house.

You open the door, slip inside. You see a woman, hands in the air, the barrel of a pistol planted in the back of her neck.

She raises her hands.

A voice asks, Who are you?

An observer.

Are you armed?

No.

Is this your house?

No.

Why are you here?

I watched the killing from Beacon Hill. Why are you here?

I'm on the run.

May I lower my hands?

The hand pulls the barrel of the gun from her neck.

Thank you.

In the faint light, You see the face of the man holding the weapon is that of a young man, a man You have seen during the debates in the early days of the campaigns—AMM 1 and BMM2.

He's after you, isn't he?

Major Magat? Yes. His hooligans, his Minor Magats. They're the ones running the killing machines.

His spokesmen said it would be a bloodless revolution....

Bloodless but only if the Progs went down quiet and

without resisting.

Are you one of the Resistance?

You mean am I a Prog?

I know you. You were in Parlezment. You were one who broke with him.

That's right. Took a stand and he wants heads in boxes and when he's collected enough of our heads he says he'll impale them on stakes on the lawn of the Residence.

What are you going to do? You're armed.

Yes I am and it has blood on it.

But you came here.

No safer place in Armendrica right now than a Magat Mansion.

After? Where will you go?

Join the others. We'll get together. Work it out. In blood. Their blood.

You knew this was coming.

Of course we knew it was coming but we couldn't strike first and we didn't know the meaning of August 24th so our timing was off but now we are up and running.

Running? They have you on the run.

It looks that way doesn't it? It looks like they hunted us down but we've turned it around on them.

How did you turn it around?

They thought they were the hunters but when they showed up, we took them down.

But you are still running.

Not on the run. Every corner masks an ambush. Every doorway hides an IED. Every window opens onto a killing field. We wait. We've got teams in control of the ammo plants in the Valley and they can't take them. No more ammo. They have ammo, but they can't get any more, not from Laurentia, and sure as hell not from Kukulkania. You'll see. It won't be long. That's why I'm here.

But you'll hang out here until…until the killing is over?

It won't be over till they run out of powder then we'll be the ones doing the killing.

So you'll hide out here until your…contacts find you?

Hide? No. Master Magat comes home and he gets a surprise he won't forget.

His stash? That's why you came here? To kill him?

No. I came here to get his stash then kill him. They're savage. You know that and you know that they make us savages because…because…you heard them read P 2025 into the Parlezmentary Record. You've heard them quote Matthew 18:6. They won't stop and that's why we staked out dozens of Magat houses in Sinverguenza…In Fierté. In Néscience and Glotona. In Vanité and Envidia. All over Armendrica…

We? You said we?

The MINO—Magat in Name Only. There were six of us on the Committee for Strategic Violence.

But you have weapons…

We knew it was coming…They've been telling us for eight years that it's coming.

The Progs were against automatic weapons.

Some were. Some still are. Some of them trained with us for the Occupied Zones pre MM1.

Trained?

You want me to spell it out? Trained for this…Clandestine ops, night-ops, blood bath training, demolition, occupying enemy fortresses. The Magats always thought that putting on camos, combat boots, running week-end warrior exercises made them killers, but when it got down to nuts and bolts, they are cowards, little whining cowards who couldn't hit a bullseye with a scattergun.

Could you have stopped it. The Culling?

What makes you think we wanted to stop it?

That's awful.

They had to show themselves. Like I said, we couldn't run preemptive strikes. But now—we've got teams out engaging.

But the thousands killed tonight, you could have stopped it.

How do you stop something if you don't know when it will start? We knew and we were ready but they pounded us on the timing.

You did nothing and now there are all the dead.

Wrong. We didn't do nothing…We did everything but pull the trigger and when our teams finish and sure the Magats might have weapons, but…and when we wrap up the major ops the violence goes mano a mano. That'll slow it down but it won't stop it until...come on, I'll show you.

DXM

He leads me into the basement of the Magat Mansion, into an armored room stocked with boxes of canned food—oats, milk, beans, flour, sugar, protein—and bottled water. Stocked as well as any grocery store. All of it labeled—Made in Armendrica by Armendricans for Armendricans. Bed rolls. Sleeping bags. Water purification systems. Foul weather gear. Cold weather gear. Even skis. In Armendrica. Skis.

They want a year's supply. In every house. A year. And there's a lot of them—each one a fortress with a storehouse for arms and food and water. The Seawenn Protocol laid it out because the Magat Planners knew it would get down to block by block and it would take more than two years to execute. You know what I mean. You've seen it.

Behind a locked steel door, on the walls racks loaded with weapons—more than I had seen in the Armory on Verguenza Avenue. Cases of ammunition marked for each of the weapons stacked on the floor.

Here you've got the loaders, AR 15s and cases of 9mm pistols. Over here you have hand grenades, RPGs and powder. Powder right now is their weakness. Without ammo, none of these weapons is worth the steel it takes to manufacture it and it all adds up to the death of democracy the Xters talk about in Matthew only you can see that there's not a millstone anywhere in this deathhouse.

He talks me through the weapons and he shows me the literature of hatred and on the wall of the Master Magat's personal armory, I see the Magat Mantra—

I am White.

I am Christian.

Your Rules don't apply to me.

I obey only the word of the Holy God and his son Jesus.

The same mantra I saw on the walls of the Great Hall of Justice and below it, another symbol I had seen only at the Major Magat rallies. MAWA. The White Christian call for the Holy God's hand to reach down and wipe the planet clean of the Darkskins.

AN APPEAL TO HEAVEN

That's on the flag the Master Magat displays outside his office in the Parlezment Building.

But not the flag of Armendrica…

You got it. They talk about pulling on the full armor of god to combat the hostile culture—meaning you and me every Libtard, Lefty and Prog. You're either on the side of god or the side of the devil, Master Magat said it pretty clear and if you're on the devil's side then just about anything can justify casting you out and that meant killing you, killing your line, your past. Everything about you will be burned. The Magats will burn you and grind your bones and scatter the pieces so there's nothing left of you—and that's what you saw tonight—genocide in the name of their Holy God and believe me, they know their Holy God is white. Not like you. Not like me. Your pigment, my pigment marks us as the children of Cain and the Magats say we're against god and that's why they're killing us all. Sorry. I get carried away when I see it spelled out.

It's all right. You had to say it. I understand, but what will you do now?

Wait.

While the Culling goes on? For how long?

Until this Master Magat gets his fill of death and comes home… to me…

YOU

You wait in the house. You listen to the young man talk to the woman and then you draw back into the shadows as a crew of six burly, bearded, big bellied White Men and their Master Magat enter the mansion. You watch as his minions—AR 15s slung across their chests—switch on the lights and in switching on the lights ignite the IED the MINO had set and there are seven dead Magats and then, on his cell phone, the MINO—a Lieutenant? A Captain? A Colonel?—makes a call and You hear a truck approach and a team of ten Progs—in blue camos—enters the mansion and in a smooth and practiced silence ferry the entire armory from the mansion to their truck and you watch as the MINO turns, at the corner, and salutes the woman who invaded the Magat Mansion.

And in that moment, You feel a sliver of hope. Hope, that dead word no one speaks in this time of Magatistic hatred. These are warriors and these warriors are serious and You know then that the Magats, in their sea of selfishness and blindness, in their desert of greed and lies and hatred had no idea what they had unleashed upon themselves. You know there will be more dying, more blood, but you also know that this war will not end the way the planners at Seawenn had worked it out. That much You know. There will be a time of deliverance, but You do not know if You will be one who witnesses it.

DXM

October. Year Two of the Culling

Each city is now two cities. Each street, each block split in two. One Red. One Blue.

No lights.

As I walk in the darkness, I am afraid, afraid for the first time in the city. I fear the streets, I feel the danger of darkness. Where once night became day, brightness banished. And the fear. Fear driven deep into the darkness so deep, so dark you don't tempt the light. And why? Prey. The Killing.

Empty streets.

Death has driven us indoors where we huddle in our own emptiness, afraid to breathe, afraid to speak, afraid of one another.

The city is a monster now. The vacant windows— eyes that look neither in nor out. Doors open to another emptiness—a hollowed out emptiness, devoid of anything we ever called joy.

Shadows. Bodies. Man? Woman? Child? Killer? Victim? Bodies skittering through the dark with insect speed, prey for the bullet sting that lingers for seconds then disappears leaving no trace. No sound.

There is a scent in the air, it is the perfume of decay and desertion, the scent of loneliness, the odor of abandonment, the smell of death seething along the city streets as blood seeped from the bodies.

And the silence as the cities eat the dead. Crack the bones of the dead. Suck the marrow from the bones of the dead. The cannibal city, the Magat dream of death—of cities built to strip the meat from bones, spit the blood into the water, drink the bloody water—the cult of the dead and dying, a nocturnal necropolis. The Xter perfect vision of the perfect world-in-waiting for the rapture that will never come but has satisfied Major Magat's thirst for blood as he waited for the tide to rise so high no dam could hold it back.

Footsteps no longer echo on the pavement.

That dark roar of engines in the night—gone. That rumble of airplanes zeroing in on the Sinverguenza airport—gone.

The city dark and the silence, the silence eats the dead. After the howl and whine of gunfire, after the curdled groans of the dying and the flaying of their skin, after there is no one left to cart away the dead—because there is no safe place to bury them— with its teeth of decay the city devours the dead, absorbs the dead a piece a day until there is nothing left of dream and hope, nothing left, not even the stench of rot, not even the spectacle of maggots who, after feasting, flitted away as dark dots into the night abandoning the dead to their bones.

DXM

October. Year Two of the Culling
The <u>B</u>ureau of <u>F</u>acts and <u>I</u>nformation

The Colonel speaks in that quiet commanding voice—the voice of a leader who has tasted gun powder, watched bodies fall in combat. She knows that the Magats have not yet recognized, will never recognize our unique position in the cosmos nor how hard it is to be human because of their belief that this is only a rest stop on a cosmic journey and at the end they will find truth in death.

Thanatopia—The deathworld the Magats created on the only blue spot in the cosmos.

October. First Year of the Culling

I bring Yaya and Yuyo to an enclave in a complex of buildings that covers two city blocks. Among the buildings there is a school. On a wall, there is a projection of a vast system of galaxies and beyond the galaxies, darkness dotted with more specks of light.

We hear a teacher talk about the uniqueness of love in the cosmos. She points to a spiral galaxy, points to a dot on one of the arms of the galaxy and she says,

This is where we live. What makes our planet special is that love and caring are unique here. The Cosmos is indifferent to us so we can't afford, if we are to survive Magatism, to be indifferent to one another. Do you know what indifferent means, Yaya? Before we evolved, there was the Cosmos, and out of the Cosmos came life and we are life but it is a lonely state of being. Do you know what loneliness is? It is our response to the immensity surrounding us, an immensity that reminds us that after we are gone—after the culling and the killing—the Cosmos continues and it will not miss us because we have paid no attention to our uniqueness. Unique. Do you know what Unique means? Think of this planet as the Lone Blue Spot in a dark and indifferent universe. We are unique, but we squander our uniqueness. What does that mean? It means that in the Magat torn Cities, the darkness of their Thanatopia reflects the dark and indifferent universe.

Thana…I don't know what that means.

Thanatopia, Yaya, is the opposite of Utopia.

I don't know what that means either.

Utopia can never exist because Utopia is an idea, a dream, a state that can never be achieved but a state that makes us want to better ourselves. That's why we call ourselves Progressives because Utopia is always a work in progress, a constant becoming but never achieved.

I see Yaya's eyes glisten as the teacher talks about the Cosmos and Utopia and Thanatopia and human imperfection and I know that now she understands every word. She says—with such authority I have to ask if she is older than sixteen—

Which means the quest for Utopia will never end but Thanatopia is right here, right now.

Yes, Yaya. That's right. Think of our planet as a spaceship. It must be Self-sufficient. Self-perpetuating. Self-contained. That is why we have to honor it. That is what we were building before the Magats figured out how to kill curiosity.

How can they kill Curiosity?

When they destroyed education. When they subverted the unions, destroyed life-science, outlawed libraries and outlawed all books but one—the one that they said had all the answers to all questions they murdered curiosity. They exiled journalists. Deported professors. Lauded and applauded ignorance. And then, the Captos led by Lord Skum and Lord Carvan wanted machines to replace humans.

Because there was more profit in machines?

Exactly, Yaya. Machines don't ask questions. Machines break down but they don't take vacations. They don't demand medical care and they never ask for a raise. Machines do what they are programmed to do and only what they are programmed to do.

Who would buy what the machines make then?

Spoken like a very wise young person, Yaya. Yes. We wanted to build a world fit for humans, but that world has to be paid for.

How do you pay for a world like that?

My, my. Yaya, your mind is working so fast. Think of it this way—If you don't have to worry about a fictional future. If you don't worry about your fictional soul you can live in this time and try to see good and to see what can be done to make the future a good place. You don't wait for *a time to come* as do the Xters with their myth of afterlife. You see? You live in the now and help build a future for those who come after you.

Before they took her, our Mama talked to me and Yuyo about greed.

Yes, greed drives the Magats. How much is enough? Has any Magat ever said they have "enough?" No. Their insatiable greed—there is never enough for them—and one day they will be stranded on their mountains, in the mountain palaces starving to death because their greed and selfishness will drive them to destroy the only place we will ever have. Do you see that picture on the wall? The one beside the photo of the galaxy? There you see the Magat Future if they continue doing it their way.

This is what their cities will become if they continue doing and living the way they are now, pulling more fossil fuels out of the earth when they know there are better ways. We teach that cities don't have to be monsters that eat people. They create cities that become monsters that eat people. How much does it take to sustain one person? Not much. We can do that, but we have to do it together.

If one of us loses, we all lose. Right?

That's right. You are so young, Yaya, so wise. Your mother taught you well. The Magats want to destroy the world but we know we can find a way to exist without killing the only Blue Spot in the Galaxy with our waste, our faith, and our greed. So. Here, we teach you to choose.

Choose to do the right thing.

Choose to see that every life doesn't have to be born.

Choose limits without crushing hope and desire.

Choose idealism without being a captive to it because an idealist is a person waiting for the technology to be born that will realize what the Idealist has been thinking.

When the Magats killed education, they killed curiosity and without curiosity—without the drive to ask Why?—there is only stagnation and despair. You are such a lucky person, Yaya. Such a lucky person.

YOU

January. Early in the Time of Infections

You return to the Office of Strategic Violence. You do not want to return because what You have seen in civilwar Armendrica is no longer strange or odd or out of place but the kinds of things You expect to see in a world that has spun free from logic and common sense. The smell of rotting flesh. The sight of human bodies reduced to garbage. The wail of women in chains, flesh ripped down to bone.

In the Office, the Colonel catches You as You stagger, stumble, flounder. Yes. Yes. All of that. Your war wounds. Your emblems of sacrifice. Your blood.

How to tell her that You have seen the dead come back to feast on the living, seen the hidden poison of death seething in the lungs of the breathing as corpses decay and release their gasses to suffocate the bound and captive Progs.

Chained together, skin and flesh sloughed off leaving the hands free, but too dead to live and the corpses fed on one another until the gases exploded and the corpses scattered.

In a warehouse—forgotten, abandoned—bodies, You tell her, chained together, stripped naked—deliberate abandonment of the living linked unto death while around the ones in chains, the twisted and bloated bodies of the black skin stretched so tight it splits spewing....

Where? She asks.

West Lake. I have never seen human bodies explode. Never smelled the stench of the near-dead swamped with the offal erupted from the dead, a smothering miasma so thick it stops the breath.

But you survived.

And wish I hadn't. Hadn't seen such deviltry—

On purpose? Of course. They took their prisoners
then forgot about them…

On purpose, abandoned them, the captive ones
chained to the strangled ones, mouths stitched shut, nostrils
pinched shut. Deliberate. Desecration.

You have to rest now.

No. If I rest, I sleep, if I sleep I dream. They trapped
the Progs then cached them with the dead and
decaying…that's what I will dream if sleep takes hold and I
don't want to dream ever again..

If you surrender, they win.

They have won. The fleshless bodies in chains are
their victory.

No. Victory is not theirs because the Pluts and the
Magats can't govern. They can blunder, they can bloviate,
they can destroy, they can rule with their edicts and their
executive orders but when it comes to governing, any ideas
they have are still-born or stolen…never their own. They
see the pathway to a future that only exists in the past. You
have to persist.

They, no one, predicted the body count, You tell
her. There is no way to haul the dead, so they left the
concrete city with the residue of killing—layers of death. I
am sick with shame and despair.

Take a deep breath, she tells You. What You have
seen is not the end of time. Thanatopia, this era, will last
only until Major Magat himself is peeled down to his bones
and the people—You and I and the others—the people will
see that under the hatred and the rage, there was only a
water-filled sac of self-deception, ignorance, and, yes,
madness. He is mad. It is an unpredictable madness. And
his people are afraid of him because he is death incarnate,
is now, has always been and will always be. He dreams of
Thanatopia but has no idea what lies beyond.

(WRITTEN ELECTION EVE NOVEMBER 4.)

OPN

November. First Year of the Culling

Yaya and Yuyo walk with me as we approach the first perimeter where a gun emplacement has a one-eighty rake of the area.

Behind the emplacement, an armored vehicle trains its weapons on the alleyways between kill boxes. Guards set up the second perimeter. First line of defense, backed by the second line of defense. No redcaps. Anywhere.

Yaya and Yuyo—bright and brilliant in a time of darkness and dread.

And I am a father teaching them how to live in a foreign country where everything is different than it was just a few months before…

What is this place? It looks like a fort.

Yaya lets go of my hand and turns away.

Come on, Yuyo, we can't be here.

Stay, Yaya. This is a safe place. This is the place we were building for you and others before the dream-killers turned it red. Before Thanatopia.

Building it for me? But not for Yuyo?

This is a world for all of you. We were building it but they, in their selfishness and their greed stopped us for a while. But we will take back the dream.

She looks at me and there is fear in her eyes, the fear you see in a child when you know the child knows you are lying to her.

And my Mother?

Flicker—The second floor, a tribunal, a white woman wearing gray prison pantaloons and jerkin. On the jerkin, in yellow capitals RACE TRAITOR.

Chin up, she stands defiant, hands at her sides. She

is barefoot.

I don't tell Yaya everything. I don't tell her about the two entire blocks cordoned off. Thirteen floors. A microcosm of the World that's in the Prog Future with its intimations of the Solerian and the Citadels.

The first floor will be the Library of Rescued Books from the Time of Burning and Banning.

Progs will hide science and the libraries from the Magats and their death-dream because Magat stupidity outweighs their ignorance. I do not tell Yaya about the Museum of Ideas that will hold all the Prog achievements.

Each floor will be a center of research or history. Each teacher will reward Curiosity.

High density arrays will power the building with a unique technology.

Ten floors below ground level—manufacturing of ideals and ideas and dreams to export to our alliances outside Armendrica to buffer them from the thanatopic vision the Magats engendered—to kill science and replace it with belief. Ideas will take root in the world of our allies where science still lives in the minds of exiles who see the future and imagine a dream of what can be while realizing that dream in Kukulkania, in Laurentia, Prerugginia, Kleisthenesia—anywhere but Armendrica. Armendrica…instead of a future for everyone…is now a nation of a greedy few living without dreams, and without dreams they have no future.

August. Year Three of the Culling

The President closed the russet-colored file, centered it on her glass-topped desk, tapped the file with her index finger. Her fingernail, pointed and painted a brilliant orange, clattered a one-two-three rhythm on the cover of the file.

She swiveled in her leather-backed near-regal desk chair and looked away, looked beyond the tall window at the span of green just-watered grass glistening in the Prerugginian summer, the far-away look of a woman troubled and curious, leery yet hopeful and knowing that what she had read was not just troublesome but the fruit of a disaster—economic, cultural, social—chaos not confined to her country, but to a broader area—the entire OBUP.

Spinning back to face the Emissary and the Ambassador, she puckered her lips and leaned forward, elbows on her desk. She said,

Ambassador, this is a report that I didn't want to read, but read it I did. You stand by all the points you raise?

Yes, Madame President. The Envoy and I spent two weeks in Armendrica with a team of specialists—

Any trouble at the border?

No, Madame President, but as you read, the frontier between Armendrica and Prerugginia is—well, it is the extension of the war-zone that is Armendrica. Every block in the city is a war zone. Every city is a war zone. The entire country is a war zone. People who once lived as neighbors now are either aligned Red or Blue and the killing is horrendous. The crux is that food is a problem because there is no Armendrican social structure other than the divided zones. No garbage pickup. No electricity. No public transportation. Bridges collapse but there is no engineering to replace them. Their agriculture no longer exists. Even the farm animals are dying. The social order has broken down.

Stop. Stop. You're telling me everything I don't want to know, Ambassador.

We have no resort but to call Armendrica what it is—a failed state with nuclear means.

President: Do I need to conference with the Armendrican Liaison.

PE: There is no Armendrican Liaison.

President: No Liaison?

PE: The Armendrican Liaison to OBUP returned home because MM has withdrawn the Armendricans from OBUP.

President: So we have no diplomatic contacts with Armendrica?

PE: Trade, of a limited and private nature, but no foodstuffs because there is no working government in Armendrica, Madame President. The Armendricans were three years in arrears with their contribution to OBUP and, according to the reports we obtain from Laurentia, Armendricans stopped collecting taxes on Day One of MM2, the day the Theocracy took hold.

Flicker—A train running at full speed onto a high trestle bridge. At halfway the bridge collapses. The train spills into the river.

President: Three years? How do they expect any cooperation from OBUP if they don't honor their commitments? How do they run their cities if they don't pay taxes?

PE: Madame President, I repeat—there is no one in charge. Once the Technos and Pluts took control and abolished taxes on the Elites, there was no work and without work there is no tax on anything. Armendrica has become a barbaric isolate. Lord Skum and Lord Caryan want that isolation. They want to get rid of all Darkskinned ones—meaning us.

Flicker—A dam on a river. Cracks in the dam leak water. A roaring, the dam breaks, water shoots through the widening cracks. A wall of water.

Flicker—A town, at night, the roar of water hitting houses. Tall buildings topple.

President: The Pluts. You're now talking the Prog dialect, Envoy. Put that aside for a moment and tell me how can they run a modern state of millions if there is no one in charge. I need to speak with the president.

PE: At the moment, Madame President, there is no president in Armendrica.

President: What? Major Magat is dead?

PE: We don't know—he might be in hiding, but no one has seen him for weeks. The only evidence that he is alive comes from the daily EOs with his signature, although no one is sure that the signature isn't Lord Skum's forgery.

Flicker—Responding to a firestorm in the center of Sinverguenza, EMTs in their ambulances and firetrucks swept away by the wall of water.

President: No president?

PE: No Madame President. There is no longer any formal political structure in Armendrica. It's not easy to explain, but if you call it as you see it you can only call it chaos.

President: Still, you arranged the Tripartite Trade Agreement with someone.

PE: There is no formal agreement, but a kind of primitive, hidden exchange and that's what I have to discuss with you before we go any further.

President: Someone has to pay to maintain the infrastructure.

PE: Madame President, I repeat—there is no one in

charge.

President: How do we pay them for our imports?

PE: In gold. Madame President. Gold. They want gold.

President: Stop right there. We can't trade gold with a failed government.

PE: And that, Madame President, is what we have to discuss. After my last visit, I walked through the process—for both leather and food stuffs, and I think we....

President: Is this going where I feel it's going?

PE: Nothing coming out of Armendrica now is what they say it is, Madame President. Up is down. Wrong is right. Light is dark. Everything is false—false labeling, false packaging. Repurposing. If you recall, the first Armendrican shipments were labeled as Pet Food, but at best, you can say everything coming out of Armendrica right now is tainted and...and I'd rather not go into details, Madame President, but the faster we act on this, the better it will be for the nation, the people, and...for you.

Ambassador: Your intuition is usually right, Madame President, and I have to say that the only thing we accomplish if we continue our relations with Armendrica is the depletion of our gold reserves. The Armendrican dhaler is worthless. They have nothing to offer. We have nothing to gain. They are running a country as though it were a business and it is a failed business because the Armendrican people have no medium of exchange.

President: You mean sever all connections? Diplomatic. Financial. Trade.

Ambassador: Madame President, let me unpack it in two words—complete uncoupling.

President: That's severe.

PE: It is severe, Madame President, but necessary. In my final report I go into detail about what I saw and what I saw is the evisceration of their once-high standards.

President: You mean?

PE: I mean Armendrica has no future until and if the Pluts and Technos are destroyed and all aspects of the P2025 reversed.

Ambassador: And quickly, Madame President. Already Kukulkania has sealed their borders after the murderous incidents involving children and…the…problem of Meat Ready to Eat…

Flicker—Armendrican refugees wearing their red caps and carrying impotent AR 15s. Sitting down on the ground, open cans of Meat Ready to Eat.

DXM

December. Year Three of the Culling

A hospital Operating Room.

A Blackwoman on the table.

A Magatte doctor is cutting out her ovaries.

In the corridor outside the OR, a line of six Blackwomen on gurneys.

I hear the Magatte doctor instruct her Magatte interns on the nature and purpose of the ovariectomy.

Castrate the blackskin males, sterilize the blackskin females.

Why not just kill them, Doctor?

You need live bodies to work on. And the Culling doesn't set well with the socialist-libtards outside of Armendrica.

The interns laugh.

Set well. Doctor?

If we kill them all, who will clean your house?

The interns smirk.

But, Doctor, dead they don't take up room, they don't use up resources.

Only the rich deserve to live. You. You close.

I watch the Magatte doctor leave the OR.

Peel off her gloves. Shake out her blond hair.

She looks through me. She looks at herself in the mirror.

I am nothing to her.

Flicker—In the high rise in Laurentia.
Julia: I have to go back.
Ryoko: If you go back I'll never see you again.
Julia: I shouldn't have left them.
Ryoko: If you go back. You die.

Flicker—Kukulkania. The border. A river. Razor-wire. Drowned Brown children hanging on the razor-wire. Laid out on the Armendrican bank of the river, a line of dead Brownskinned children. A band of the Magat-Pride, flaying knives in hand, works its way down the bank skinning the dead children. The Magat-Pride tosses the skinned bodies into the bed of a dump-truck. Stacks the skins on pallets.

Flicker—a slaughterhouse, beheaded, skinned human bodies hanging from hooks.
Flicker—A peelatorium in a meat packing house in the Fremont District. Black men hang from chains. Hispanics. Asians. Eight bearded white Minor Magats wearing plaid shirts, boots, Magat hats are eating lunch. Lunch is peanut butter sandwiches, a slice of Armendrican cheese
Magat One: Les git started on them brownies.

DXM

September. Year Two of the Culling

I watch two of the burly, bearded, big-bellied men hook the chain binding the feet of a Darkskin man and raise him, head down, then with razors peel his skin while he screams and kicks.

Minor Magat Two: God damn spic son of a bitch, hold still you immie faggot.

Flicker—scar-face man sitting, mirror in hand, peels the skin from his face then gnaws at the skin.

September. Year Three of the Culling

The Prime Minister, standing at a window overlooking the Laurentian River glanced at the reflections of her two agents, standing hands clasped behind their backs. The women with cropped black hair wore black suits accented with simple white dickies. A single silver service lapel pin with Laurentian colors. Black flats. The PM faced the agents. She said,

Never understood it. Studied it in school, in uni, made a world-wide study of parliaments and governments but even now I don't understand it.

A tragedy it is, Madame Prime Minister. Without even a signature on a piece of paper, but by fiat and directive, Major Magat and his elite pluts changed Armendrica from a democracy to a theocracy.

MM's signature on a piece of paper and blood flows.

And is still flowing.

How strong are we at the border?

We have infiltrated agents into the tent cities. Daily figures are in the minister's reports. We have stripped them of their weapons, taken control of any ammunition flow and checked each of them—man, woman, child—for disease and contagions.

Is that enough?

Madame Prime Minister?

Yes Cyringa?

Many of them are illiterate.

The children?

And the adults. No basic understanding of calculations.

Arithmetic?

Nothing. Many of them can't sign their name except with an X and have no idea of anything beyond rudimentary language.

And the tattoos, Madame Prime Minister. The
males especially, have body tattoos of a range but most of
them connect to or reference a date....

The Prime Minister opened a desk-drawer and drew
out a red folder that she spread on her desk. She said,

Like these?

The agents, as one, leaned in to check a list. The
Prime Minister admired the hands of the women as they
leaned over the desk. A single ring—as if they were
twins—on the right ring finger, fingers with plain but
polished nails. Single women. Accomplished. Polished.
Cultured women. Laurentian women. Educated. Free.
Fearless.

White Choice, the Only Choice
MAGA
MAWA
Make Armendrica White Again
Down with Brown
Vermin Poison our Blood
I am White.
I am Christian.
Your rules don't apply to me.
Lock'em up
OK. OK.OK.
4/20
13/51
1488
J6

Day One

Yes. Most of the dates, but only one or two with the
Hakenkreuz and that usually hidden on the body. The
favorites are 4/20....

Hitler's birthday, the Prime Minister said.

J6 and Day One.

J 6 The date of the first insurrection. Day One the date of the Capitulation.

And MAWA…Make Armendrica White Again.

1488 is especially troublesome…

That one appears only on the right hand fingers of white males.

And that makes it more troublesome. If an ideologue sports 1488, it means that he is committed to the fascist doctrine and P 2025 practice…

Yes, Madame Prime Minister. Our infils report that the 1488s carry out much of the Culling and so as you'd expect an inordinate number of the refugees carry that sign.

We will never allow them into Laurentia, but of course borders aren't one hundred percent secure so we have to accept that these illegal 1488s are already in Laurentia. Do they know we have decoded their signs?

Some have tried to lase their tattoos, but our infils know not to question or remark, so, if at some later time we need to, we can move without any trouble.

Yes. Better to watch them than to drive them into hiding. How are your infils situated with the Progs in Armendrica?

The Progs are staying in the cities. They know who we are and where we are and they are especially targeting the Magats who carried out the genocide and…

All that entails—we don't need to go into that here, now. I think that will be all. Oh. One last item…the laser tags…

Every immie who presents at the crossing is tagged, named and dated. We know where they are and who their contacts are meeting with. That kind of surveillance is expensive, Madame Prime Minister, but… It has to be done and it will be done. Those who cross….Do you foresee any action of the kind that turned Sinverguenza and Verguenza

into cannibal cities?
Here? In Laurentia?
Yes. Here.
No Madame Prime Minister. We are still civilized.

DXM

May. Year Two of the Culling

I am there when the trucks roll into the warehouse on Conception Drive. Conception Drive—what's left of the last the Medical Center where, before the Culling, before Major Magat's justices legalized crime, women found the relief they needed. The Medical Center was once a pristine, stainless steel and porcelain facility but the Antis turned it into a pregnancy rescue station after the MJs criminalized the right to choose that once guaranteed women control of their bodies.

Then the Culling began and all of that changed in one day.

I follow the trucks into the basement where the medical equipment is stacked and useless against the walls and on the walls floodlit Anti-banners—

> ABORTION KILLS CHILDREN
> CHOOSE LIFE
> I AM WHITE, I AM CHRISTIAN
> YOUR RULES DON'T APPLY TO ME

I watch bulky, burly, bearded White Magats steam-strip labels from cans—

> PET FOOD
> NOT FOR HUMAN CONSUMPTION

and run the now naked cans—quart cans, pint cans, half-pint cans—through a relabeling machine—

> MEAT READY TO EAT
> MADE IN ARMENDRICA

The relabeled cans roll down a conveyor to a packager that boxes twelve cans into cartons, each carton with a shipping label—Prerugginia Humanitarian Aid or Kleisthenesia Humanitarian Disaster Aid—then sends it to a stacker where two Minor Magats—white men, bearded men, burly men—Minor Magats—wearing camo gear, boots, and the signature red hats with the lettering MAKE ARMENDRICA WHITE AGAIN sewn onto them—load the cartons into trucks.

When each truck is stacked and packed, the Minor Magats take a break before hitting the process again.

MM 1—Them Immies…

MM 2—Major Magat says they come here just to poison our blood.

MM 1—Kinda funny, ain't it?

MM 2—What's funny?

MM 1—Darkies eatin' dark meat.

MM 2—Yeah. No. Yeah. The best dark meat. Made in Armendrica.

MM 1—I need a smoke. You got any butts?

MM 2—No. Had to hang up the smokes.

MM 1—The doc say you come down with somethin'?

MM 2—Nah. Got to hittin' the pipe. Had to throw it in.

MM 1—Oh, that's bad shit, bro. Immies bring that shit in like it's candy.

MM 2—Let me tell you, kickin' it took more guts than you get in a peelatorium.

MM 1—That's funny, ma-man.

MM 2—Kinda, huh?

MM 1—Kinda worried.

MM 2—'Bout?

MM1—They get onto us, hi-gradin' the…uh…

MM 2—Don't bother your purty little head, we got protection.

MM 1—Protection? I don't see no 15 strapped on your skinny ass.

MM 2—Goes way past 15s dude. Goes higher than your paygrade.

MM 1—No shit?

MM 2—Absofuckinlootly. Where you think that five hundred you're gettin' comes from?

MM 1—I mean…

MM 2—That's right. You get it now?

MM 1—The Pride.

MM 2—Hell no. The Pride. Who do you think pays the Pride?

MM 1—What?

MM 2—Like I say way past your paygrade. There's Technos rich enough to buy the Holy God but we gotta get back at it if we're gonna meet the quota. Another load backin' in. Son of a bitch, I hate having to work.

MM 1—Maybe Major Magat shouldna deported all the negroes back to Africkastan and all the brownies back to Coocoolandia.

MM 2—Kukulkania.

MM 1—Coocoowhatia?

MM 2—Kukulkania. They call it Kukulkania.

MM 1—That's what they call it?

MM 2—Yes. Kukulkania.

MM 1—And this Coocookania's where all the dusky vermin come that's poisoning our blood?

MM 2—That's what Major Magat says, yes. But he says he's gonna annex it and call it an Armendrican state.

MM 1—I heard Major Magat's dead.

MM 2—More of your conspiracy theories.

MM 1—No, I heard it.

MM 2—Scuttlebutt. All lies. Major Magat's gonna live forever.

MM 1—Yeah you're right. If he was dead we wouldna gotny work and how dya like them spuds?

I hear another truck at the loading dock.
A semi.
The quota.

Flicker—A peelatorium. Bodies hanging stripped of their skin. White men with flaying knives carve at the bodies. Business-like. Smoking.

I watch the Minor Magats trudge back to the labeling machine, to the cartons, to the canning machines. This time there are hundreds of cartons of cans rolling on the conveyor belt to the steam stripper.

PET FOOD
NOT FOR HUMAN CONSUMPTION

Outside, I breathe thick air, feel the weight of corruption in it. I remember the world before the Culling, before the pillage and rape of the future, before the death of curiosity, the world we wanted to build—a world where no person, nation, color had to live in fear. Diversity. Progressive Diversity. The Rainbow. All of us, each of us. All gone.

FLICKER—a gold plated sedan. Black leather seats._ A Shantung-suited Master Magat criminal boss sits at the wheel of the sedan. Two uniformed Border Magats approach.

October. Year Two of the Culling

The Shantung silk suited Master Magat in his gold plated sedan—sunglasses shading his eyes in the pallor of anemic street lights—smokes a cigar. Standing outside the sedan, a Border Magat, his blue uniform with the ABP logo—an image of a steel mesh fence—sewn on the shoulder, speaks, his voice a throaty whisper.

BM—Getta thousand a day, sometimes more. Depends on the Kukulkanians.

MM—Coocoocanians?

BM—Kukulkanians. South of the Rio.

MM—Ah. The Rio.

He flicks his cigar ash out the window, brushing the Border Magat's arm. The Border Magat looks like a grandfather—gray hair, slight paunch, baggy uniform, boots scuffed.

BM—Might can move just shy of a dozen ever coupla days.

MM—Can or will?

BM—Depends. Pet food for wetbacks don't seem like it's right.

MM—Wetbacks havta eat. Your cut's thirty percent.

BM—Thirty percent?

MM—This is good meat, cowboy.

BM—Don't know, sir. Lotta hands tween here and there.

MM—Forty percent. You work out the split.

BM—I gotta whale of a crew.

MM—Fifty percent. That's it.

BM—All right then. Fifty percent.

MM—First delivery in three days. Okay?

BM—Gotta be then.

MM—You and your team gotta relabel the meat before…

BM—I get it.

MM—Can you handle that?

BM—My team can handle it.

The Master Magat tosses his cigar out the window of his gold-plated sedan. The Border Magat crushes the butt under the heel of his boot. I watch the Master Magat drive into the night and I imagine what the Border Magat does in his spare time. If he is a grandfather, he has grandchildren. What do they think of his work? Do they know anything about what he does? Is there a grandmother for the grandchildren? Does she work? Is she a Magat Mother? The Magats butchered the Black Grannies because without books, the Granny is the last link to the past, the foundation of memory, the cornerstone of culture. Grannies gone, the children are rudderless. Grannies gone, there is no one to teach history to the children. The Magat goal, after the Seawenn Protocol, has been not just the eradication of the Blackskins in real time, but the complete deracination of Black culture as a way to erase the stains of slavery. The Magats learned their lessons from history. Never admit any wrongdoing. Never atone. Never agree to testify. Mask the past behind a wall of hatred in the present.

DXM

April. Year Three of the Culling

I follow the Prerugginian Envoy into the meat packing factory. She is tall, dark-skinned, dark hair, a gliding smooth walk. She has an air, a presence, a directness that reminds me of a woman who reads deeper into the mind of the other to reveal more than the other cares to reveal. I am certain we could become friends if I ever met her but I am invisible. In the beginning, I was worried about my invisibility, but Jay created me to be silent, to observe, to comment only when I had to. The more familiar I became with his style of writing, I saw what he was doing as a writer and I am now happy to work the inside, to speak in the Oracular voice that OPN uses—the distancing from the action to comment on the action—a choral figure uninvolved but deep and observant and able to point out the weakness and issues with Magatism and politics and how politics have entered into the meat producing and exporting system.

The PE has no idea that what she is looking at is human. The Master Magat has learned his patter well and even though Major Magat denies knowing anything about Seawenn or P 2025, it is evident that this Master Magat, a salesman born with a silver tongue, has worked out the details and that he knows two things—he knows to the minute what stage of the process is underway and he knows how to lie and make the lie sound like fact.

MM—From here the rail carries the haunches to the cooking center where it is heated to 375 degrees F and then cooled, stripped from the bone and canned. We expect your deliveries will be on time.

PE—The meat looks funny.

MM—That's because we have only Prime cuts

here—lean meat, no fillers, low fat, no additives, just the purest, finest dark meat available.

PE—Still looks funny.

MM—Are you a hunter, Your Honor?

PE—Hunter? You mean do I track down animals and kill them?

MM—Yes, your Honor. We call that hunting.

PE—No. I have never hunted—anything. We gave up hunting in Prerugginia centuries ago.

MM—Then you aren't familiar with meat as good as this meat. You see, when you hunt a wild animal, that animal always has a low fat level because in the wild the animals are not pen-fed, say the way geese are forced to eat—that's what gives you pâté de foie gras—and so the meat has less fat, hence less marbling, and it gives you that 'wild' taste' that you find in—say elk, or deer. But this meat….

PE—So low fat makes your meat look funny. And why do you hunt wild animals when you have the means, as you said you would show us, that….

MM—I understand, Your Honor, but you can trust me when I tell you that the stages of preparation are unique to Armendrica. Here you see only the bone-in unbutchered meat. You are probably more familiar with the final stages—the grading and the cutting followed by the packaging and finally, distribution—and distribution is what shows up in your market. And let me tell you that all the meat from this facility is Prime Grade. You won't find any finer, better dark meat than our Prime.

PE—So you will ship only these…uh…haunches to Prerugginia?

MM—Absolutely, Your Honor. The lesser cuts— the chuck and the brisket and the shank, we process and package in a different plant and that we ship as pet food. The famous Armendrican Pet Food. 'Only the Best for Your Pet.'

PE—Pet food? For dogs and cats.

MM—And for zoo animals, Your Honor. Lions, tigers, hyenas, cheetahs.

PE—Cheetahs? Cheetahs don't exist now.

MM—Yes, I'm afraid we lost the last of our cheetahs when the progs forced us to close the Sinverguenza Zoo, Your Honor. That was the year we had to repatriate most of the captive animals.

PE—Repatriate?

MM—I mean return to the wild.

PE—Where in the wild? Where in Armendrica is there the *wild*?

MM—The progs and their democratic view of the animal world, you know.

PE—Where do you raise this meat now?

MM—In special areas where we cull the herds and select only the finest specimens who produce the best meat.

PE—Again, what kind of meat is this?

MM—It's the haunches, Your Honor. Only the haunches.

PE—I see. Haunches. What kind of haunches? The meat looks funny. Where do you raise it?

MM—Your Honor, there is nothing to worry about. Trust me. If you and your entourage care to go with me, we can visit the tasting room.

PE—Tasting room?

MM—Before any batch of meat leaves this facility we run extensive quality control procedures. The tasters sample the batch and if it's not absolutely first rate, out it goes. You see? We in Armendrica take great pride in our abilities to groom, raise, and export A-1 products.

Yes... Made in Armendrica is a guarantee of the finest, best, most selected meat outside of the Pampas. Now, if you'll follow me, I will guide you to the secondary facility where we tan the hides. The Tannery. You see, Your Honor, in this day and age, it doesn't make sense to

waste any part of an animal. In the tannery, you will see the
system at its finest—turning the freshly peeled hides into
the finest, softest leather, Armendrican leather. You know
our motto—'Leather so soft that you can almost hear it
breathe.'

April. Year Three of the Culling

From the slaughterhouse, the Master Magat leads the Prerugginian Envoy to the tasting room where the tasters—six of them—sit at a table. On the table, open cans of meat with the label—
MEAT READY TO EAT
MADE IN ARMENDRICA
The tasters—all young Darkskinned women—wear white smocks. Hair nets. White gloves. They are manacled to the tables where they work.
PE—One question, Master Magat, sir.
MM—Of course.
PE—The bones.
MM—The bones?
PE—What about the bones?
MM—Uh. Oh. The bones. Yes. They go to the bone crushers—that's in another facility where the bone crushers pulverize them, turn them into bone powder that we then export as fertilizer…bonemeal…for worms…enrich the soil, you see?
PE—Do you export bonemeal to Prerugginia?
MM—Oh yes. And Kleisthenesia.
PE—And Laurentia? And all the Occupied Zones as well?
MM—We have an envoy, much like yourself in Laurentia to set up a Board of Trade Agreement, but Laurentia, well, they're socialists and you know what that means.
PE—So our food—if we ratify the deal—will grow from the same bones that the meat you're packaging for us comes from?
MM—That is absolutely correct, Your Honor. Guaranteed product made from the finest resources humans can make. You know our motto—Made in Armendrica— from the ground up. First class meat, first class bone meal.

PE—One last question, Master Magat—why are the tasters manacled?

MM—Well, of course, the manacles…uh…you understand, that the tasters…uh…well…the tasters are convicts waiting for…uh…sentencing….

Flicker—a line of manacled Darkskinned young women wearing white hijabs and gloves enters a peelatorium. Herding them are two burly bearded big-bellied Minor Magats armed with whips.

MM—git in there, you ugly brownie cunts.

DXM

March. Year Three of the Culling

I follow the Kukulkanian Emissary to Armendrica to her briefing of the President of Kukulkania to explain the situation at the rio and the refugee camps.

KE: They stormed the wall, Madame President, but we turned them back. They are demanding that we supply them with ammunition so that they can return to Orgullo and continue to wage their insurgency.

KP: Numbers?

KE: In the thousands, Madame President. I don't think we should honor their demands because it is the red caps who began the culling, as they call it.

KP: You were stationed for several years in Armendrica before MM1.

KE: Yes Madame President. I was in Armendrica City when Major Magat floated the idea of annexing Kukulkania and turning it into an Armendrican state.

KP: I recall the moment. Yes. Another of those uncoupled, disastrous MM ideas.

KE: Armendricans elected him, Madame President.

KP: They aren't very smart are they, these Magats?

KE: When a state abolishes education it's what you'd expect.

KP: Do you see any…hope?

KE: Hope? No, Madame President. I returned to Kukulkania the day MM declared by fiat that Women were subhuman creatures who have a place only in the church, in the kitchen, or on their backs and pregnant with their mouths open.

KP: Yes, I recall the problems that MM caused our diplomatic corps. And yet, here I am, president of Kukulkania and I'm not on my back. What do you recommend?

KE: Quid pro quo, Madame President.

KP: Meaning?

KE: Give them nothing. Do not give them ammunition for their weapons, do not allow them to cross into Kukulkania because their ideas are poison and that poison is not only contagious, it is destructive, it is…in a word, zani.

KP: You are fierce. Not one iota of support for these…Magatized-Armendricans? The meat ready to eat people?

KE: Outrageous, Madame President. That they think they can export such barbaric products and expect us to accept them. Before? Not now. Not one iota of support for these…

KP: Is it actually…the meat of….

KE: Oh yes. I have the assays, Madame President. DNA evidence shows us that their canned meat is human.

KP: What do you need? Do you have contacts in Armendrica we can exploit to keep abreast of conditions and…the future…

KE: Right now, Madame President, the future is not a pleasant place for Armendricans. Years of…no other way to say it…of slaughter. OBUP is calling it genocide. I recommend further that we void all trade agreements, nationalize any factory held and run by Armendrican Pluts, and to finish the job, deport every Armendrican who violated the crossing AMM2.

KP: Is that the wisest position to take, Emissary?

KE: Not just the wisest, Madame President, it is the only position to take. As I recall at your first meeting, MM shouted at you and said he wouldn't sit at a table with any woman who is childless and has only cats in her house.

KP: Oh yes. That was another of his disconnected rants. Hilarious.

KE: That isn't all, Madame President. These immies from Armendrica, they are ignorant, uneducated, superstitious, bigoted and hate all Darkskinned people.

KP: All Darkskinned people yet, they assume that they can convert everyone around them to see the light of their jesus…

KE: While they reduce women to a state of servitude. In short, Madame President, we don't want them and their poison here. And one last item—that white jesus.

KP: White? Now that is laughable. Don't they know anything?

KE: As I said, their ignorance is matched only by their stupidity.

KP: All right. About the meat.

KE: The meat?

KP: We need origins and names to attach to the meat. Names and places. Times and Names. This is history, Emissary, and we have a duty to document it as well as we can…We have learned from the past, we remember the past, and we will not let the past dictate our present.

KE: Not easy, Madame President. In the beginning, the 1488s kept names and places, but later, as prescribed in their P2025 document, they destroyed all evidence.

KP: There must be at least shreds that we can send to the world court if we bring charges of genocide against the Armendricans.

KE: Not much remains, Madame President—except the Skins, of course, but…as the Magats say, 'plausible deniability cleanses all skins.' I've checked with the Bureau of Facts and Information, but even they draw blanks—no one knows how many Blackskins died, were skinned, males castrated, women sterilized and…served.

KP: Served…Oh my. All right. I'll have Balham draw up the withdrawal papers and you may present them to the proper authorities.

KE: That will not be easy, Madame President. There is no proper authority in Armendrica at this time. Every city from Sinverguenza to Verguenza to Orgullo to

Fierté is hard divided and fortified. They are self-contained as were the ancient city-states but now it's city within city.

KP: Fortified? Divided? Entire cities? Still?

KE: Yes. Armendrica is, at the moment, a failed state. The progs have maintained control of some of the important manufacturing, but even they are tainted with the repugnant policies of the residual MM corrupted Parlezment.

KP: How do we proceed, Emissary?

KE: Through our Kleisthenesian connections, Madame President. They are the last members of OBUP who maintain contact with the ad-hoc Parlezment and I am certain that contact will dry up very, very soon.

KP: This is disturbing, Emissary. Armendrica once was such a lovely land full of hope and dreams.

KE: Yes, Madame President, but stupidity and ignorance cannot replace hope and dreams. Ignorance is in their blood.

KP: Is any of this forgivable? After all, they are, how shall I say it, recent arrivals. Last millennium they came as conquerors and they destroyed five thousand years of our science and myth and murdered millions of our ancestors.

KE: And now they are working to murder our second millennium.

KP: One more question and then I'll let you go. Is it true that they eat their dead?

KE: Madame President. I can't tell if that expression is hyperbole or fact, metaphor or fiction, but one of the recent curses that has come out of Armendrica is 'the flesh of your mother sticks in my teeth.'

KP: That sounds definitive.

KE: But only a linguist can decode it.

KP: Decode it?

KE: With the Armendricans and the way they sexualize everything, it might have a sexual innuendo.

KP: Are you sure of all this?

KE: A white jesus, and the flesh of your mother, Madame President? Yes.

KP: You'll have the papers later tonight.

November. Year Two of the Culling

I am in a cage-room in a peelatorium with dozens of older Black Women. They are the Grannies. They are naked. Two armed Minor Magats—bandoliers with only a dozen cartridges, no 15s—stand outside the cage laughing.

A Minor Magat opens the cage and one by one leads the Women into the Culling Room where a dozen bodies hang from hooks on a flat plate monorail—carcasses ready for the Culling. The Women do not wail. They do now cower. They stand straight—I have seen this before, seen it in the unsanctioned tribunals when the Women—White, Brown, Black, Yellow, Red—stood defiant as the Minor Magats passed their foregone judgments, sentencing the Women to Death by Butchery in the Courts of the Armendrican Right-Wing. Red-loving, Zani, Major Magat worshipping killers answering the call to Make Armendrica White Again.

One by one, clubbed in the head the way a butcher kills cattle, the Women fall—to their knees, on their bellies, on their sides, and the Minor Magats hook the Achilles tendon of each leg of each Woman, and hoist each body onto the rail that carries the bodies to the Culling where, with knives once used to gut and skin animals, the Minor Magat butchery begins.

And all that time, the Grannies, each one defiant in death, do not scream or shout or cry.

I watch the Minor Magats, gleeful in their work, first slice open the belly of each Granny, then with quick slashes, cut the entrails loose to tumble to the conveyor belt that carries the offal away as waste.

Each body passes then to another Minor Magat who flays the carcass leaving the meat—red meat, red blood, each and every one the same—ready for the Minor Magat butchers who cut first the arms, then the haunches then the legs until the only parts of each body left on the hooks are the feet. The body, now meat, no longer a human, rides out of the peelatorium to the cannery—a factory within a factory—where it will become Pet Food—Not For Human Consumption.

And then, I see the Minor Magats march back to the Cage, open the cage gate, but now there are no more Women.

There is only blood and skins.

Skins stacked a dozen at a time onto a conveyor—murder now industrialized into routine—that carries the skins to the tannery.

Sickened, I leave. I walk into the cool air of the Armendrican afternoon and I remember times before the Culling when to take a breath of fresh air was renewing, invigorating, peaceful. But now, in the hellish Magat-zani world of the Culling, there is no peace, only interludes of no death. No peace, but there is a wailing—a wailing you feel more than hear. It is a high and mournful and crushing wail, a lament that grows with each body culled from the rest of humanity—what there is left of humanity in this Magat time—only because of the color of their skin.

I understand then, as clear as anyone can ever see it, that the Seawenn Protocol has one tenet—to destroy not just the Black, the Brown, the Yellow, the Red—but to eradicate every trace of their existence. Fascism. Zaniism. White Christian Nationalism. Magatism. Thanatopia. Make Armendrica White Again…

The Master Magats know that the allomother is the key to the annihilation of the Blackskins. The Master Magats know that with the Grannies gone, the Blackskin children are easy prey—sex, drugs, crime…easy to kill.

And now, here, the grandfather, Border Magats selling meat. Pet food. To Kukulkanian immigrants. Pet food relabeled.

The final solution. The brutal final solution—to kill and skin the blacks then butcher them and package their meat as Humanitarian Aid then ship the meat to Prerugginia and Kleisthenesia and to the Occupied Zones and to the camps at the borders with Kukulkania where Immies eat the meat offered to them… Humanitarian Aid. The Magat Plan to feed the world….

DXM

In the beginning, they hunted us. Man or woman wearing the rainbow or the color blue, blue as sure a target as a flock of birds—they hunted us—

Armed with their AR 15s, the ammosexuals, wielded their Wilson Combat automatic pistols with religious fervor. They stalked and destroyed whole sections of the cities, turning them into deserts. Houses empty. Bodies lying for weeks where they were killed.

In the beginning, the Magats shot and killed women, children—white, black, brown, yellow, red—it made no difference—anyone in blue, even those who did not resist. Later they took us prisoner to the show-trial tribunals where they tried, convicted, and sentenced us to death because we wore blue, because we were Libtards, Lefties. Progs.

We were race traitors. Sex traitors. We were women who had rejected the Holy God of the evangelists. We were women who loved women. Women who lived with men of color. Women who bore children with men of color. And with each sentencing, each bullet to the head, they chanted—

We are White. We are Christian.
Your rules do not apply to us.

Flicker—At the tribunal where the GLPs sit in

judgment. Greedy little pukes, incel, insane GLPs who, in their ignorance of history, kowtow to the image of Major Magat and complain about the price of gasoline and the cost of lettuce.

DXM

In a Prog House, in a desk, in a notebook I found this account of a First Encounter—a firsthand report of the first times. There is only one outlet now for this writing because MM and Lord Skum have Xed out, outlawed the internet. They have banned all sources of "fake news," which we know now is anything that criticizes either one of them—MM or LS. I will talk to OPN about this piece— maybe find a spot on the darkweb—but it's hard now because the ops have to keep changing location, ISP, and I know that MM and his Master Magats are trolling for the darkweb and, of course, the penalty for either of us—OPN or me—will be a peelatorium. Still. I have to get it out because this is the writing that will show historians the truth of the Thanatopia that MM and LS built with their cruelty and hatred. The writing of this woman will tell the Laurentians and the Kleisthenesians and the Kukulkanians how unprepared we were for Day One. It shames me to think that we knew it was coming. Magats told us it was coming, but we didn't want to hear it. The one great weakness of a *Libtard*—not wanting to believe that the Magat's main job is to kill you.

August.
It was dawn when they came to my street.
I heard them coming, I heard gunshots. Screams.
And as I looked out, I saw Ellen Kole, my neighbor, on the grass, a red-capped Minor Magat standing over her, his AR 15 in her mouth and I saw him pull the trigger.
On the ground beside Ellen, Peter Kole, a boy of

fifteen, on his belly, hands behind his back.

And the Magat shot him in the head.

That was when I ran.

We knew it—first the Killing, then the Culling—was coming. From Day One Major Magat told us—in his tirades before the election, and after, we knew it was coming, but we did not want it to come as it did. Early on, I had put together a Go-bag with a coat, money, water, and I ran. The weapon—a Desert Eagle. Still hanging there on a hook in the closet. Useless.

I knew it was a mistake to leave the weapon hanging in my closet. I was not alone. Not alone. There were millions of us ready—not to run, but to fight—and I should have stood with them instead of letting the Minor Magats run over us for as long as they did. I don't know how many times I listened to them rave about Libtards and Pinkos and Commies but I never spoke up...until now.

If anyone ever finds and reads this, I want you to share it in anyway you can. I will not be here. I am going out, taking my pistol and my supplies and I am going to the Inner City where I know there are no Zanis. Zanis. The Minor Magats have their leader, the orange clown, the snake-oil salesman whose crimes will one day catch up with him and then we will see the truth but the Zanis—the acolytes of Lord Skum—are a different breed. Their zaniism is never hidden, was never occult, and because of it the Culling went deeper than anyone ever thought it would. And I am one who takes the blame. The others like me who heard but didn't listen...wouldn't listen because none of us imagined the depth of the depravity lurking in the minds of the zanis and magats.

Flicker—Interior a Minor Magat house. A Magat sits face to face with a woman. He says, Got to have more babies to keep the blackies from out-breeding us.

Flicker—A young girl sits with a Magat Preacher. He strokes her hair, her belly. She looks at him. Tearful. He runs his hand up her thigh, between her legs. She closes her eyes and bites her lip.

Flicker—A judge in his robes in his chambers on his desk, a can of meat Ready to Eat. He opens the can. He smells the meat.

DXM

April. Year Two of the Culling

I have been here before—on a bench outside the Magat Judge's chambers—where two Border Magats wait. They are anxious. I see it in the tremor of their hands as they wait. The younger one looks at his fingernails. He glances at an opening door.

A Magat Clerk in a doorway.

The judge will see you now.

The BMs follow the clerk into the chambers where the Judge sits at a desk reading. The Magat Judge has a fringe of gray hair. Pattern baldness. His pate glistens in the overhead light. He has a full white beard.

He wears a stenciled crimson T-shirt stencil printed in bold white lettering.

I EAT LIBTARDS

The Magat Clerk exits, closing the door behind her.

The BMs stand. Obey in Advance. Silent. Do not speak. Magat-world.

The Judge finishes reading. Looks up. His eyes are a seething hot red. Puffy bags under the reptilian eyes.

What do you dingleberries think you're doing?

Well, your honor…

Don't *your honor* me, you idiot. You go behind my back and I find out about it three days after the first delivery.

I guess we wasn't thinking, Sir.

What did he offer you?

Offer, sir?

Let me lay it out for you, officer— meat Ready to Eat.

Oh, you mean for the immies, sir.

The immies. Yes.

Fifty percent.

Fifty percent.

Yes, sir.

The Magat Judge rears back in his chair. He folds his hands over his T-shirt. Closes his eyes. Rocks. Then he leans forward.

That's a pretty hefty cut, fifty percent.

We work hard, sir. It takes time, it takes…well…fifty percent…

When you walk out that door, you leave twenty-five percent on this desk.

Twenty-five? We gotta eat, sir.

Maybe I'll boil you and eat you…

We ain't libtards, your…Sir.

What are you, officer?

Just a guy trying to make a living. These are hard times, sir. The Chief he takes fifty percent, you take twenty five percent, that leaves me doling out shit to my troops just so we can build up a little reserve cause we got mouths to feed and when everything goes to hell…

Watch your language, officer.

The Judge turns a plague around.

Read it, officer.

I am white. I am Christian.

Your rules don't apply to me.

I obey only the word of the Holy god.

I apologize, sir. I don't know what got into me.

Twenty-five on every can, every delivery, every week and remember this—I've got eyes all over you and this operation so don't get greedy…or…else…I'll skin you and your mute sidekick here.

Yes, sir.

A military wheel. The two Border Magats march out of the chambers.

The Magat Clerk, arms across her chest, stands in

the hallway.

I follow the Border Magat home. He carries a can of Pet Food. A car in front of his house seems to puzzle him.

At the door, he hesitates. He peers through the window, takes a deep breath, and then enters the house. As always, I am alone watching, waiting. I ask myself what he is thinking holding that can of pet food—soon to be relabeled and hawked as meat Ready to Eat, Product of Armendrica—and knowing that the MJ and the man in the Shantung silk suit are taking a piece of his profits leaving him with what?

In the living room, he stops. On the sofa, his daughter. Judi—a teenager with long black hair. A jewel, she is. She wears a pink smock. She is barefoot. Beside her, the preacher sits holding her hand. He looks up at the Border Magat.

BM—What's going on here, Judi? Maud? What's going on?

MW—It's Judi. She's…uh…not well.

BM—Not well? What's the reverend doing here? She need a doctor?

MP—Too late.

Judi looks at the Border Magat, her father, and she bows her head.

Judi—I'm sorry, Daddy.

BM—Sorry? Sorry for what, baby?

MP—Your daughter has sinned. Not once, not twice, but three times.

BM—She's thirteen. She's just a child.

MP—No sir, by the Holy God, she's a woman and she has sinned and she has to pay for her sins.

BM—How much?

MP—What?

BM—How much do you want to wipe away her sin…whatever it is.

MW—It's not that simple, Dad.

BM—What's she wearing? That thing?

MW—It's a hospital smock, Dad.

BM—A smock? Why's she wearing a smock? First time I seen a smock on her.

MW—It's my fault, Dad.

BM—What's your fault?

MW—I made her do it.

I look at the girl, at the mother, at the father, at the preacher and I do not like what I see but there is nothing I can do, nothing I can say. I can only watch and listen. I know. I have seen it before.

MP—Your daughter is the spawn of Satan and your wife, her mother is the instrument of evil who gave her unto Satan. And she, your wife, and she, your daughter, must pay the price for their sins.

BM—What the heck are you spouting that for?

MP—Sin is sin and where there is sin, there must be reparation.

BM—How much?

MP—The price is heavy, my friend.

MW—He says we have to die, Dad.

I have seen the flesh of girls like Judi—innocent jewels as only young women are jewels until that moment when they cross into the dark world that men, such as the preacher, promising light and happiness, lead them into. The preacher—now sits in judgment of Mother and Daughter.

BM—Judi?

Judi—I'm sorry, Daddy.

BM—Maud?

MW—Judi…was…pregnant, Dad, and she…

MP—Had an abortion. Abortion. Abomination. And…

BM—Judi? What? When?

MW—I knew, Dad. It's my fault.

BM—Who?

Judi—I…don't know for sure, Daddy. Not for sure.

The Border Magat kneels. He looks at his wife, at his daughter, at the preacher. He still holds the can of pet food. He sets the can on the floor at the feet of his daughter. I am wary of this. Under that single hand movement, there is anger, there is fear, there is violence and I expect to see the Border Magat explode. But…

He bows his head. He takes his daughter's hand.

BM—Was he a prog, sweetie? Tell me he was a prog and I'll find him and I'll skin him alive and make him pay for what he done to you. Tell me he was a prog.

Judi looks startled. She looks at her mother. Then at the preacher.

Judi—I don't want to die, Daddy.

MP—But she has taken a life. She is a child of Satan and she is a murderer and she must pay.

BM—How much?

I watch the preacher draw back, a smile on his lips, his chin lifted in haughty indignity.

MP—You think you can buy the Holy God's forgiveness.

MW—I'll tell you who he is, Daddy.

The BM glances at the mother. I see his eye lids flutter.

MW—That's why he's here. He's here because Judi told me when she…first showed…and I had to think about it, because I can't let my daughter suffer because of what he has done.

BM—He?

MW—Yes.

BM—He is the father? He did this to our child?

The Magat Preacher stands. Throws back his head. His lips fixed in a snarl.

BM—You? You are the….father?

MW—Dad, don't.

BM—Sin? She sinned? You sinned. You. You

sinned with my daughter and you want her to die because she…

MP—It is not I who demands atonement. Her sin is murder. It is the Holy God who wills it. She killed a child that was a child of the Holy God and that is the sin she must sacrifice her life for.

MW—Dad. Don't. Don't. Please? Don't.

BM—And my wife? You defile my daughter and you say my wife must sacrifice herself for your sins? Fornication? With my child?

MW—I took her…

BM—Took her?

MW—To the…place…

BM—The place?

MW—The clinic.

MP—That is the price the Holy God demands. That prog place is the den of iniquity and sin. It is a slaughterhouse defiling the blood of the Holy God and your wife is the instrument of death and your daughter is the spawn of Satan and they must atone. Now.

BM—No. They. Don't.

MP—Read the Holy Bible. It is clear and evident and there has to be retribution and if you stand in the way you know the price you will pay. There is no doubt. We are white. We are Christian. The rules of Armendrica do not apply to us. We obey only the words of the one and Holy God. Do not question the words and the words of the Holy God are that she must atone for her sin.

I wait. I watch. I listen. The Border Magat, still kneeling, bows his head. Defeat in the slope of the back, the bare neck as if waiting for the execution itself there, in his living room. The can of pet food—for the immies at the border, exported to Prerugginia, Kleisthenesia, Kukulkania—glistens.

Then, the Preacher stands. He picks up the can of pet food. He says,

The Committee will come here and take them away. If you stand in the way, they will take you too for rebelling against the Holy God and his word.

He walks out of the house, into the night. I hear his car drive away.

In the silence, the Border Magat stands looking at his wife and daughter. He says,

Pack up, Maud. You and Judi pack up everything you need for a long stay.

Where are we going, Daddy?

Laurentia, Judi. We're going to Laurentia.

He turns, stiff, military, and he goes to a closet and he takes out a pistol in a holster that he straps on and then he pulls out a shotgun that he checks for load and then he faces his daughter. He says,

There's no place for humans in Armendrica now, Judi. Lords Skum and Seashol are monsters and liars and thieves.

But Jesus, Daddy.

Jesus wouldn't recognize Armendrica, Judi. The Zanis have turned it upside down. Come on. Hurry. We have a long way to go tonight.

Is there any hope, Daddy?

Forget about hope, Judi. We're running for our lives now.

But. My friends?

We won't be alone, Judi. Thousands like us have had enough. We have to get out.

I follow them into the Armendrican night. How do I write a story about a family of three disappearing into the fog and forget and I have to ask myself how many others will take the same road. Is he right, the Border Magat? Is there any hope left in Armendrica? Any hope at all? Do I have to write hope's obituary here? Hope, the last thread of decency and its extinction in the Thanatopia Major Magat Seashol and Lord Skum created?

DXM

April. Year Two of the Culling

I rode with the team in the back of a truck. Twenty men—Progs, outfitted in camo, boots, balaclavas—carrying Benelli close-quarter shotguns, weapons they had taken from Magats late in the killing after the Progs realized that pacifism, mollification, even moderation were three words for death.

The Progs look at me. I'm used to the gaze—being there, being everywhere at the same time. I am proud of what I do. Not the thing you want to hear from a woman—pride—in a world that just two years before had women on their knees or on their backs waiting. Always that waiting.

It was night. These were night ops and the ride was rough and long and brutal but there was so much at stake.

An extraction, they called it.

A rescue op.

The target—bodies.

Men and women captured in Magat raids, stolen from their houses, kidnapped from women's health clinics and held captive in peelatoria where they waited, in chains, in cells, for their verdicts.

Prog 1—ten to go. Check your gear.

One by one the Progs cleared their weapons. I heard a sigh, the long, collective sighing of armed men on a mission that might end in blood and meat and bone, but a mission that meant so much to the women—the doctors, the PAs, the techs who risked their lives to help women and girls.

Prog 1—Count off.

One by one the Progs called their numbers then fell silent as the truck turned and the bodies swayed all in one direction.

Prog 1—Two squads, front back. Got it?

As one, twenty men spoke. Got it.

The stop.

The silence.

That collective sighing again…

The Prog leader pulled back the flap and the men, their Benellis in hand, dropped out of the truck, silent men, big men with purpose in every move.

An act of revenge?

An act of mercy?

An act of war?

All of that—now practiced, ingrained, returning terror to the Zanis with the same power that the Zanis had turned it on the men and women in blue. How many times had I heard it—this civil war will not be about borders and territory but about neighbors and minds.

I followed the lead team of ten down a narrow street to a building that I knew well—it once had been a high school. In the rage and panic of the first two years of the Culling, the Magats turned it into a peelatorium.

It is amazing how big men, carrying heavy weapons and wearing combat gear, can move in silence, the only sound the rush of air into excited lungs, the release of the air, the quick but quiet brush of arm against side and then the leader kicks in the door and eleven bodies crash into the gymnasium and what I see is sickening—stacks of skin, black skin, even in the low light of the dimmed down gymnasium I see black, and on hooks, hanging head down bodies—black men, black women—blood dripping into barrels—and then the first shouting and the silence is no longer and there is the booming of the Benellis and the cries and screams of men with legs shattered, heads split with the slugs from the M4s, and I follow the Progs into the middle of the gym and there, in cages, I see what we came for—bodies of men and women and children, white bodies, black bodies, brown bodies—naked bodies waiting for the knife, the hook, the gutting, but the Progs now move as one cutting down the Magats as they rise from their cots and their bags, their clothes the clothes of death defiled with the blood and gristle of their victims and they reach for weapons but it is too late, much too late as the ten back-up Progs burst into the gym taking down the crew of Magats until all of them lie either dead and on the gym floor or on their knees hands behind their heads whining don't shoot, don't shoot, don't shoot.

Prog 1—Secure?

Prog 2—All secure.

Prog 3—Motherfucking chicken-shit murdering sons of bitches.

The Progs open the cages, bodies move in slow motion and in the eyes of the bodies, I see the dark chasm of fear give up its darkness to the light of release and relief and there is sobbing, their nakedness the purity of hope and at the freeing, I understand nakedness.

Prog 1—Into the cages. Drag their dead with them.

Herding the Magats—now naked, barefoot, dirty, bloody, pulling their dead into the cages—the Progs, M4s pointed at the naked men, stand back.

And I understand nakedness.

Prog 1—Lock'em in.

Prog 4—The Skins?

Prog 1—Have to leave them.

Prog 2—Seems wrong, Chief.

Prog 1—Get a cleanup team in here. Check for IDs. Take what you can.

A team sorts through the stacks of clothing along the walls of the gym, looking for paper any paper—driver's license, Medical card. Library card, Any document that will identify any of the cut and butchered and desecrated bodies in the peelatorium.

Prog 2—And get some clothes on these people.

Prog 1—Head out, load'em up.

The naked clothed, the dead Magats in their cages,

the living leave the gym and in the journey back to the truck there is silence broken only by the mutterings of thanks and the silent nod of the head from the Progs and I see the faint sheen of tears on the cheeks of armed men and I understand how nakedness reveals the utter truth about what we have become and it is only in the moments of nakedness that we show our shame.

In the truck, in the crowded truck, the body heat isn't what it should be. It is as though now safe, the bodies—the black men, the black women, the white women, the white men—have lost something very important. Lost something that has a name but cannot be spoken in the silent aftermath of killing.

DXM

April. Year Two of the Culling
—Six hours after Extraction

It is quiet in the sanctuary. Silent and calm and after the storm of the rescue, the freeing, the rumbling of the truck on the war-torn streets, the tranquility of time settles in the way a warm blanket eases the pain of surgery. And the women, safe now but still bowing their heads as they sit on the cots while the doctors tend to them—to their visible wounds, and I know that nothing can soothe the hidden anguish, the pain of their humiliation that the women exude, humiliation, a disease oozing from the body—the terror of the screaming now past.

I sit facing her—LouRachelle is her name—but she can't raise her eyes to mine so I wait. I have learned to wait, now, in this time of blood and bleeding, learned the second, third and fourth meanings of the word *wait*. And as I wait, I look at her, watch her, see the pulse in her neck of her still beating heart, watch the rise and fall of her now life-giving lungs in her chest. I know that the body in front of me—black and beautiful, and touchable—had, just hours before, been doomed to destruction and in that moment, I catch my breath, clogged up in my throat, in my chest, solid as a hunk of metal as the images of LouRachelle flash in my memory to the moment of the cutting of the chains and I remember the sudden light in her eyes—the light of an animal freed at last from the trap holding her captive—not yet understanding either the why or the how of the springe.

Can you tell me how it happened?

She looks at me with animal eyes and her lips move but she can't bring herself to utter the words that live in her.

LouRachelle, I am a writer, a reporter, a journalist…I am a survivor. I have lived with the blood and

the bones of others for two years now and I told their
stories and now I need to know yours. I need to know
because someone has to write it down for later…later…
when…when and if there is a future and the monsters come
to trial and they will come to trial...

Why you? Who are you? Why do you want to
know?

The abrupt rupture of her silence shatters the pain
lingering in my chest and I feel myself lifting—she lives.
She has broken free.

Someone has to tell your story, LouRachelle. What
you tell me will stay hidden until the time comes to reveal
the truth.

The truth? In Armendrica? A journalist? Truth? No
one knows what to believe in Armendrica. No one believed
you in MM 1, who will believe you now?

They, the Magats, would have killed you. That's
truth. Truth everyone should know. They would have
skinned you. That's truth. Truth that not one of the Magat
justices would have saved you because Major Magat
Seashol and his Technoautocrats write the law. That's
truth….Someone has to speak before the Magats destroy
every Darkskin in Armendrica…

She looks at me. I wait. I don't know now how to
read beneath the anger, the pain and fear. In Armendrica all
emotions have melded into one snarled mix of human
anguish. *I'm scared.* I have heard those words so many
times. *I'm scared.*

All right. I was in the clinic when they came. The
sanctuary. There were others there, you know…A girl.
With her mother…

You Know. Words that have a special meaning—not
an assurance, or a pause, but history… KNOW…I know
that the skin she wears was a single slit of the flensing knife
from destruction and her body a minute away from
becoming meat…and as she speaks, I write the flowering of

her story.

I'm a doctor but that didn't matter when they came to take her. They took all of us—nurses, doctors, girls, mothers—calling us all criminals, race traitors, half-breeds. And the doctors took the worst beatings…I can't…I thought I could, but…I can't…I saw the Magats with their knives…

The rush of memory flooding through her bows her neck—and I can only imagine the weight on her, how heavy the seconds of life must be to a woman who has stood on the verge of extinction, a victim at the whim of a man's anger and hatred and stupidity.

It's over, LouRachelle.

As I speak her name, she comes back, she looks at me, and in those now watery black eyes, there is a spark that fades in an instant and she shakes her head.

No. It will never be over—for her, the girl. Judi.

Judi? You know her name?

They can't have a family name. You know that. You know.

Yes. I know. But you are here now. Safe.

Why me?

Don't do that to yourself. Don't ask that question because no one can answer it...

She struggles with that word….

We…we…*I.* Couldn't stop them from taking her. Thirteen…she told me

Listen to me, LouRachelle. There are questions but there are no answers because no one should ever ask those questions of a woman…not by anyone, anywhere, ever.…

You think you are being kind. I look at you…and…

I know…my skin, my pigment, my blood…just like yours and yet here I am…while you almost were not.…

The father came with them. A horrid creature. A preacher. The Mother called him Reverend, but he was full of hate and filth shouting that the child by coming there had betrayed the Holy God and she will forever bear the mark of Satan.

Again, the bowing of the neck, the submission to time and place and history, that bowing is the surrender to hatred, never to look into the eyes of the hater knowing that to look into hatred is to look into death…you own death…and how can a single glance, the arrow of a gaze lead to annihilation?

I'm not here to preach, LouRachelle. I am here to help you, to tell you, to show you that we…

I hate that word…*We*…we did nothing.

But we need that word, and you know we need it because…

Because….no one can explain it. You know that.

Yes. I know that. One man, a selfish monster says one word—kill—and the world whirls into a blood-letting savagery and they take you…no matter who you are…no matter what you have been and done and for who you have done it…it doesn't matter…they take you…Me…

I don't hate anyone.

I know. I know.

And that's why.

Why? I feel ill right now.

I'll bring someone to look at you.

Not that kind of ill. Deeper than the body ill.

That illness.

I need to sleep, at least to rest before I get back on my feet and go back to work.

Can you? Go back to work? After this?

If I don't, who will? These girls need me, need us. I know she will die. He will kill her and kill the mother.

She shudders then. She sags.

It isn't the weight of life on her shoulders pulling her down, but the knowing. Knowledge can have a weight way past its heft, as if we can weigh knowing. Knowing what? That what has happened, what is happening is possible? And the why—because one man says one word and the believers not knowing anything past that word bring death and in the bringing there is the nonsensical death of the bleeding and killing. And it goes on and on and on.

LouRachelle lies back on the cot, curled up into that ball we all know as the sanctuary of innocence, as if curling up, erases all the past where comes a moment of the new beginning.

I cover her with a woolen blanket. A gray woolen blanket stitched with the words *Property of the Armendrican Republic*...a relic from a time now gone, a time never again to be.

Her breathing is slow and soft and regular, but her fists are clenched and I know that the return she hopes for will not be the return she finds.

Leaving the sanctuary, I cross paths with the Prog leader.

How is she?

In pain.

He looks at me. I watch his eyes flicker over me, eyes that rake and raze with a hard gaze that just a year before would not have been there. And then, a quick smile.

She okay?

Yes. Okay.

Not good?

Not so good.

But okay?

Yeah. Okay.

Some of the others aren't so okay.

Takes time to get over what they saw there.

Maybe they'll never get over what they saw there.

His smile dissolves into a hard, wrinkled mouth and he takes a deep breath.

Can't get over it.

Get over it?

How we fucked up. So bad. Let'em take over knowing what they were gonna do to us.

You can't undo any of that. Take it easy on yourself.

He looks at me, the hard gaze back in his eyes.

Don't like what it's done to me.

You saved more than you hurt.

Huh.

No. Really. That girl. Those women.

Those women. Yeah. Those women.

Those women have nothing against you.

No. You'll write about this, right? Write it down so no one will forget that it happened? Write it down so no one later's gonna say it didn't happen, 'cause it happened. All of it happened and you have to get it down.

I'll get it down.

Don't like what I see when we go on these raids. Gotta ask how many we don't save. Gotta save'em. Can't save'em. All.

DXM

April. Year Four of the Culling

Never apart, always a part, I watch the Prog drive the flint shard into the Magat's face, red cap flying. The bone breaks through his skin, through the back of his skull with a sharp crack.

He falls. On his back.

The Prog, machete in hand, cuts the Magat's throat.

Silent. The whisper of steel slicing through flesh, through bone.

And then he stands.

Holding the hairy head of the Magat he spins into a bayonet in the hands of a charging Magat. The bayonet slices open his belly. The trophy-head flies loose from his hand.

Fucking prog.

The Magat yanks the bayonet from the bleeding Prog, pokes at the corpse crumpled on the ground. I watch his eyes scour the street—the bodies on the street, the stones, the knives, steel sharpened into lances—and I remember OPN telling me the day we entered the ammunition manufacturing plant—Let them have their 15s. If they can't shoot it, it's just a club.

And here they are…Magats using rifles as clubs to fight Progs fighting with rocks. This is what Major Magat's Thanatopia has become—men with rocks and clubs killing one another. In four years, Major Magat has not made Armendrica great again. He has driven Armendrica into a Stone Age.

The Magat puckers his forehead until it shrivels into a dried prune. Inhuman now. A killing machine. Leaving the dead for the city to eat.

The Prog dead.

His blue cap askew on the street.

His blood. His bone.

He lays beside his prey.

Not much left to fight for is there?

The Magat looks through me. I am not there. To him. I'm never there.

Not much left to fight for.

This blackass libtard's dead. If I'd had a 15 there'd be a hundred of those blackskins dead right there.

You got 15s in the Armory.

Libtards got'em locked down.

Your friend? The red cap?

Let'im rot. Let'em all rot.

He looks through me. Walks away. Fist clenched. Bayonet dangling.

Do you call this a win?

He does not turn. He walks toward Freedom Platz with the measured stride of a man on his way to a funeral.

I, You, He, We…The We no longer exists in Armendrica. There is only I in the cities of the dead.

Flicker—Three stylish Magattes sitting at a café table. Coffee. Cake. Dark glasses. Each woman wears an eye-shielding broad-brimmed hat that complements her outfit.

June. Year Two of the Culling

I took Yaya and Yuyo to an abandoned Magat Mansion on Suffolk. In the basement, behind a brick façade, in a hidden compartment the Master Magat had stacked survival supplies—cases of dried milk, dried eggs, protein caps, cans of rice, survival rations containing ready-to-eat dinners, twenty five-gallon jugs of water complete with purification tablets and emergency water-straws. And behind the water supplies, a locked chest.

Yuyo broke the lock, lifted the cover and took out an AR 15, five full clips of .50 caliber Beowulf ammunition and a reloader with powder and bullets.

I'd leave that alone, Yuyo.

Did the Magat who lived here kill anyone with this?

I don't know.

Of course he did, Yuyo, the Magats all hunted Blackskins.

It looks new.

Yuyo set the 15 on the table, settled in at the ornate baroque table with its matching chairs. Cutting a meal-packet open using an SRK like the one I had carried.

I can't eat.

Why can't you eat, Yaya?

Because I can't eat if I have to look at that.

She pointed to a framed painting on the wall.

It was the standard portrait of Major Magat as God, Jesus Christ, and Hitler rolled into one, complete with radiant cape, fur collar, gold sneakers.

His hair the color of spoiled carrots, his skin dyed the putrescent color of a corpse left on the ground for a week.

Bloodless.

With the SRK, Yuyo sliced the portrait from its

frame, cut it into eight pieces that he stacked on the altar and stabbed the stack of canvases with the knife.

Thank you, Yuyo.

As they ate, I watched them.

They ate in silence.

They drank in silence from the water jugs.

Finished, Yaya pushed away from the table. Looked at me.

Mister, did everyone know that Major Magat was a mole?

A mole, Yaya?

In school, before they shut down our school, some of the kids were saying that Major Magat was a traitor and mole for the Bear and that everything he owned including his palace, the Bear had paid for. They said that Major Magat wasn't even Armendrican.

That's what people were saying, Yaya but I don't know.

You know everything, so why didn't you know that about Major Magat?

There are many things I don't know.

Did you know that in our school, some trans kids killed themselves because the Magats taunted them and called them fairies and non-human?

Yes. I know that.

Did they peel the ones they caught after The Culling started?

Yes. They had peelatoria for Trans kids too.

I had friends who were Blackskins and being Blackskin and Trans and kids told them they should kill themselves because they were abomynations? What is abomynations?

You mean abomination, Yuyo. That's what the Magat kids had been taught to say. Blackskin abomination. Trans abomination. Yellowskin abomination. They learned it at school and at church and at home.

At church?
Yes. At church. And at home.

Flicker—a park street in the Park District. The street is empty. The plants and trees are desiccated as corpses. The grass, unmown, waves in the slight breeze. Spotted deep in the grass, bones. Disarticulated bones. Skeletons that only the grass can bury.

YOU

July. Year Two of the Culling

Late, one night, You go out only at night now. The only exercise You get in the night and its darkness is the only shield You have from the debased and bloody Magat City that once lived in the light of the minds of thinkers and artists, of poets and writers, a City that now lives in the night-fear of death. Thanatopia. The death-city of the Holy White God.

Through a window, You see a Magat family at their dinner table. You enter. You see the Magat Mom. You listen to the Magat Patriarch talk to the boy who is crying.

MP—Josh, knock off that bellyaching or I give you something to bellyache about.

Josh continues to cry but tries to choke it back.

MP—slaps him in the head.

MP—What did I tell you? You knock off that blubbering, you little shit.

MMom—He's just a kid, Dad.

MP—You. You shut your mouth. I want anything outta you, I slap it outta you.

You follow the Mmom as she leaves the table, goes to the kitchen where she fingers a butcher knife. Looks out at the MP and her son. Her son now sits, head bowed. MP lights a cigarette, smokes it. Then, in disgust, crushes it in the dinner plate.

MMom looks away, looks at her ring finger, the diamond ring on the finger.

She returns to the table, picks up the MP's plate with the cigarette butt.

MP—Say you forgot to say your prayers for Major Magat. Say it.

Josh nods. He looks up. I see his eyes. Red.

MMom—Do what The Father says, Josh.

Josh looks at Mmom. Lowers his head. Yes.

MP—You know what means, son?

Josh nods.

MP—Go get it. Right now. Go get it.

Josh stands. Crying, he leaves the table.

MP—What the hell is wrong with that kid, Mother?

Josh returns carrying a leather strap with a bronze buckle. Hands it to the MP then still crying bends over. I watch the MP walk around the table. He stands behind the boy.

MP—Drop'em.

Josh shucks his pants. The father raises the strap, the bronze buckle zings against the boy's bare bottom. Josh yelps.

MP—Say it.

MP raises the belt.

Josh—I am White.

MP strikes Josh again. Josh screams.

Josh—I am Christian.

MP raises the belt again. The buckle flashes and digs into Josh's behind.

Josh—Your rules don't apply to me.

MP—Finish it.

He raises the belt.

Josh—I obey only the word of the Holy god and his son Jesus.

The MP smiles. He turns to the Mmom.

MP—You useless cunt. You gave me one, just one and then you dried up into this worthless sack of shit I have to look at every day. And you know what? I'll tell you what, the Black bastards are outbreeding us and that makes me the good guy 'cause Major Magat's sure about that— when we're through there won't be any blackskins in Armendrica. Still. I ought to get rid of you. Why don't you just die? You die and I'll find me a real woman—a woman who's ripe and full not all dried up.

Mmom—I'm sorry.

MP—You're worthless. If you couldn't cook, I'd kill you.

DXM

July. Year Three of the Culling

I eaves drop on the three entitled, privileged Magattes at the table in the café on Main Street. With my back to them, I am invisible. They talk as if they are the only humans in the café. I take notes. Notes, because one day, Major Magat will die and with him will die embryonic Magatism and I will have a record of the past. In their words. Words filed away in my stash of history. OPN has warned me that putting together a history can be dangerous…but how else can I show my disgust? I listen—

He humiliates her.

(Note: Her. Must be Major Magats's mate.)

Did you see how he tried to kiss her and she turned away?

Those lips, I wouldn't let him touch me anywhere with those lips.

Touch you? Anywhere? Not even…

(Note: Risqué talk for three Magattes.)

What do you think I am?

How does she stand it? The shame?

She gets a lot out of it, you know. Married to Major Magat and all that power.

His power doesn't do her any good.

Could you say no to him?

Would you invite her to tea?

Tea? Really? You…

She only goes out when he makes her.

Power soothes all shame.

Yes, and what she gets is only veiled admiration…

And only one child after all those years. Do you think she…

Either that or she's had an abortion.

Oh harsh. Either that or she never lets him…you

know.

No. We don't know. Tell us what you mean...

(Note: Laughter.)

Well, he must weigh a ton. And that business with that woman. You know, the one who spilled it all and said he isn't...well. Enormous...

(Note: Laughter.)

Hypocrisy is what she gets from the hypocritical monsters in the Residence. Can you imagine what it would be like with Mister Master Magat Mueller?

(Note: Giggles. I hear the clink of spoons on cups.)

I heard he doesn't....

Do it very well?

(Note: Whispering. I hear only three words...)

Back door man.

That's how the third most powerful one gets it?

(Note: Giggles.)

Or takes it.

Oh, so you know about *that* back door?

Don't you?

Would you let him?

Could you refuse him?

I have to go. So glad we could get together. Next week?

Flicker—An eight-foot iron-mesh fence around Parlezment. Magat bodies hang from the fence. Inside the fence, the Parlezmentarians in their rainbow flak jackets. Armed with high-power weapons. RPGs. M240s. The weapons used in the former Occupied Zones.

YOU

November. Year Four of the Culling

You enter the Parlezment Building, a neo-classical-Greek/Roman-Revival-Modernist-Post-LeCorbusier with Frank Lloyd-Wright flourishes and Neo-Baroque ornamentation.

Parlezment is everything that once was Armendrican.

A fusion.

A conglomeration of culture, time, space, ideals, liberty before Technoautocratic Fascist White Christian Nationalism turned politics into a deflated idealistic balloon and crashed the Wall.

When the Magats came the first time and in force, the Parlezmentarians had not learned the lessons of realpolitik, had not learned to yank hard on the neck-chains of the lobbyist-culture, had not learned to shorten the reach of the plutocratic-privileged-entitled Technocapitalists, had not torn off the black robes of the judicial traitors and in that failed to demonize Major Magat and so did not return him to his criminal state, did not send him to prison.

And You watched the blood lettings and the castrations. And You knew that Armendrica was lost. Lost. You know now how it feels when a nation loses its spine.

This time, when the Magats came, they expected the Libtard-Dem-Prog coalition to lie down and submit to the massacre.

Not this time.

RPGs primed. M240s loaded. And the Libtard-Dem-Prog fighters knew how to use them.

You were there.

The second time.

The Magats came in waves, waving their flags and their banners, brazen with zeal, the Minor Magat minion shine in their blood-letting eyes.

And they died.

This time, they died.

And from his hidey-hole in his gold-plated plantation at the extreme border of Armendrica and the ocean, Major Magat Mister Seashol incited them still to kill.

But this time, it was different.

The Armendrican Armed Forces had cleared the neo-zani-fascists from the ranks and turned the turncoats out and this time when the Minor Magats came with lightning in their hands they met with thunder on the left and it was fearsome and they died.

In numbers.

And they drew back, bloody. Armendrican blood spilling Armendrican blood, the attacks repelled, they turned then to the streets.

They found the Wall had thickened. The skin of the Libtard-Prog-Dems had thickened. And this time, the Progs did not feel guilty about the guns they kept in their closets. Not this time. This time the split was so deep, the hatred so violent, that there was no choice but to fight. So primitive it was fight or die. The Minor Magats, as their thought-masters had coached them, believed they had the armed right and holy might of the holy god in their hands and he would through them exterminate their enemies but this time, the Progs and the Dems and the Libtards fought.

They fought. And You watched them. And You read about them—about the blood they sacrificed, about the limbs and bodies and minds they laid open as they reclaimed the streets and the houses and brought civilization back from the darkness and in the law found ways to rip control of what was left of Armendrica from the Magats—the Major, the Masters, the Minors, Lord Skum, the Pluts and the Captos and the Silken-suited and Lord Caryan and his army of Technoautocrats—and make them pay for the blood-letting.

You watched the defeated retreating Minor Magats run in the streets, watched them crash into the walls they had built, barrel into the barriers they had built between houses and the barriers—that had divided the streets, the cities, the nation—came down.

Flicker—Ravenna Boulevard. Barricades. Burly, bulky bearded white Minor Magats armed with AR 15s at the barrier.

Posted on walls, on light standards—No coloreds past University Avenue. Make Armendrica White Again.

Flicker—A high school gymnasium in Middletown.

DXM

October. Year Two of the Culling

Four young, thin, shaven, shiny Minor Magats
wearing dark glasses—dressed in white polo shirts, khakis,
shiny black leather oxfords—sit on the stage at a high table
looking down at a bound Black man and a Black woman.
Behind the four Magats, a flag hangs from the wall.
Over the flag the Magat Mantra in flaming red lettering—

I am White.
I am Christian.
Your Rules don't apply to me.
I obey only the word of the Holy God and his son Jesus.

The black man is enormous. 6' 6" 300 lbs.
Head shaved.
Naked.
In chains.
The black woman is thin. Heavy-breasted.
Head shaved.
She holds her hands over her delta.
She glares at the sitting Magats.
Magat 1: Where did they round up this buck?
Magat 2: This darky was one of the Hawks.
Magat 1: Hawks. Used to be a white man's game.
Look at it now. Nothing but Blackskins. Even got
Blackskins coaching white boys. What's your name, boy?
Black Man: James.
Magat 1: I mean what's your slave name boy?
James: I am Armendrican. I don't have a slave
name.
Magat 2: All you blacks got your African name.
Magat 3: What are we ever going to do with you,
James?

Magat 1: Look at the size of that buck's dick.

Magat 4: That dick has to come off.

Magat 1: Must have been in a lot of white pussy.

Magat 4: No more white pussy for this boy.

Magat 2: You know what we've got for you, boy?

James: It'll take more than four of you pukes to do it.

Magat 1: This boy's got some fight left in him.

Magat 2: Let's see how he looks with hooks in his shanks.

Magat 3: I think I saw this darky play.

Magat 2: What? You paid money to watch this monkey?

Magat 3: I think he played defense with the Rams.

Magat 2: No matter. His playing days are behind him.

Magat 3: Answer the question, boy. You know what we're got for you?

James: I know.

Magat 1: Peelatorium.

Magat 2: Yes, but first, my fine-feathered friend we castrate you. You know what that means?

James: I know what it means.

Magat 2: And then we decapitate you.

Magat 3: The female too.

Magat 2: You want her first?

Magat 4: You get first cut at it.

Magat 1: First cut? That's good.

Magat 2: I'm not touching that skanky cunt.

Magat 4: You gotta start sometime, somewhere or are you waiting for white meat?

Magat 2: Not interested in any kind of meat.

I hear the incel in his voice. Thick. Racist. Misogynist. The voice of a once beautiful young man now a woman-hater, a race-theorist doomed to live his solitary life on the outside—no family except the incel family. The

Pride. The Creativity Movement. Where race is his
religion.

*Flicker—A peelatorium. Screams. Shouts. Stacks of
skin—Asian skin. Brown skin. Black skin. Peeled bodies all
look the same.*

*One by one, a team of bulky, big-bellied, bearded
Magat butchers quarters the peeled bodies and with
precise, practiced cuts, strips meat from bone and tosses
the meat onto a conveyor belt.*

*Flicker—Fierté—a row of houses on Lakeshore
Drive. Side by side with Armendrican flags, rainbow flags
flutter in front of each house,*

OPN

December. Year One of the Culling

I am ashamed. I wrote this editorial but didn't post it. If a writer doesn't write from the Truth, doesn't write from the heart, then the writing is always in the service of the Captos—the Lords of Words who think they own the language and will kill the Critique, slaughter the Truth-tellers. I save this now for later—if there is a later. As I watch the Magats spawn their P 2025, I remember Medved's Plan to cleanse his country of all the Brownskins using viruses and poisons designed for specific gene pools. Make Armendrica White Again has its roots in the Bear's insidious plots. P 2025 sounds like the bastard child of that sick Medved and his caste of killers. This is what I wrote: "Murder. On a massive scale, you expect reports of atrocities and excess. Good news is no news, and without the press—and Major Magat has gutted the press to the point that you, the reader, do not believe one word in print—and with the conspiracy mentality that has infected the brains of most Armendricans, there is little credible reporting keeping the pipelines free of those atrocities and excesses, so you gloss over the chaos and the genocide as something alien, something not us, something made up. History rewritten, history adjusted, crippled and maimed. The suspect alternative reality the Magats feed you.

"But when you find maimed people, injured people, people to talk to, you hear stories, tales, experiences of the excess, the extremes—you hear the Truth. And you have to own up to what you have done and you have to ask why you have done it.

"Even before the Culling, Armendricans had little respect for the press and now, in the time of blood-letting and its racial horror, you have still less, but once you hear words loaded with more than a kernel of truth you are challenged.

"You know truth when you hear those words coming out under pressure, words thick with that eye-blinking near-to-tears state that only pure truth can squeeze from a human. Those are the words that I write. The words that DXM writes not because we want to but because we have to. They say that in war the first casualty is Truth. And in the Culling that was Truth. Major Magat Seashol spoke and Truth had become Lie and the few who dared contradict him vanished—banished? Or murdered? Victims of the MMPPS, the Pride, the Faith Keepers—Brown shirts all acting behind the shield Major Magat and his capto-plutocratic coterie of billionaires built."

DXM

She—I don't write her name because the Magat Justices freed the Minor Magats from all restraints when they dissolved the Armendrican Constitution and enshrined Major Magat on his golden throne, so if some Minor Magat stumbles on this document—no matter how well I hide or disguise it—She will die.

She agreed to talk to me, but her words come slow as if each sentence is torture. She sits on a chair. Knees together. Imprisoned in fear. She looks at me and in her eyes there is that darkness that lives in the eyes of survivors.

Late November, She says,

And then, She tears up. Lips quivering, head-bowed.

And I wait.

She takes a deep breath and again She looks at me now with the same look She projected to the camera when She was on the air—and She says,

They murdered eight secret service agents. Right

there in the studio, with Major Magat watching them.

She stops to take that extraordinary breath pain and anguish and wonder and horror all share.

Who murdered them?

His MMPPS, the Black Shirt secret private protection army he bought before the election. They were always there, always with him every time I had him on, and I had to have him on the show because his billionaires owned the show, owned the network, owned me, owned what I said. It was do what they tell me to do or be banished—like you were banished and who and what am I without my show? My show is me…but now…now… I didn't know, nobody knew but they came out of the Pride. They were the ones who organized the first insurrection that drove the ELPs out of Parlezment and into hiding. They were the ones who hunted down the ELPs and slaughtered them just the way he said he would slaughter them.

I hand her a glass of water.

I wait.

She pulls herself together and then after a sip of water, She says,

If he finds out that I'm talking to you he'll send them after me but I have to get it out, you have to get it out. He's so vindictive. Anyone who crosses him, anyone who says no, he'll kill. You know that, don't you? And the Magat Justices set it up for him. They knew. All the Pluts and Captos knew what he would do and they let him. Oh. At first, I thought…I believed the vulpine voices feeding me their truth but now…I can't…

I've read Timothy. I know.

This goes beyond Timothy. This is horror, this corruption…Only the vilest dictator orders this kind of killing and you know no one will tell him no…ever. This is the end…if you keep these recordings…never let anyone hear or see them…not until…until…I don't know…until we…find a way to bring…Major Magat…to justice.

I watch her in her despair and I remember listening in the early days of the regime when Major Magat Seashol tore through the Constitution demanding that Parlezment back down and rewrite it and I think about the day I watched him sell out the nation to the Silk-suited men, men with clean hands, men who never had to apologize or rationalize because they knew that Major Magat had given them everything they wanted—blood and money and power—and…She had gloried in that time as well, every time She had him on her show…but now…here She is, sitting with me crying about the murder and blood She knew was coming…

DXM

January. Year Two of the Culling

The house stands in the middle of the block. At first it looks like an ordinary house—new paint, three floors, solar panels strung on the roof. A heat pump hums. But then I see the barricades disguised as planter boxes and I see the gun slots in the barricades and in the gun slots the barrels of machineguns. This is a fort. Barricaded. Fortified.

I enter the house along with a cluster of battle-scarred troops—Liberals, Leftists. Some White, some Brown, some Black. In uniform, some of them torn, bloody.

I show my press card to a helmeted Prog guard who pats me down.

In a large room three Progs in battle gear sit at a conference table covered with maps, some rolled, some spread. The crew I entered with stands until the three leaders finish their talk.

Then, the Colonel asks where they were from.

We just came from the battle in the Central Market.

We heard about it.

It didn't go well, Colonel.

Magats?

We got word that they'd rounded up the last of the ELPs from Parlezment and had herded them down to that Peelatorium in that Youth Club they'd commandeered. We tracked them, thought we'd cut'em loose and bring them back here knowing you'd have an idea of what to do with them but the MMPPs ambushed us at the Peelatorium.

You took the ELPs out?

Not exactly. Got a couple of Minor Magats but another squad of Magats lit into us—MMPPs—and that's when it went all to hell. What're we gonna do when they

keep killing and cutting? They can't kill'em all, can they?
That's what breaks our balls…

*Flicker—One the wall of a Prog House, a portrait
of Major Magat as a naked fat clown with carrot curls for
hair.*

Major Magat tells them to kill as many as the Holy
God wills.
I can't get over how they knew where we were.
Took you by surprise?
Total surprise.
What happened out there on the street?
No bullets for the 15s. So it came down to the
blade.
Let me ask you a question, Sergeant…
Shoot, Major.
What did you have in your closet on August 24th?
In my closet?
In your closet.
Camping equipment. Mountain gear. Scuba tanks.
Camping equipment. That's why the Magats think
we're pussies and wimps and cowards. That's why they
think they can take us down and skin us. That's why they
went after Parlezment the second time…

*Flicker—An eight-foot iron-mesh fence around
Parlezment. Red-capped Magat bodies hang from the
fence.*

…you play chess, Sergeant?
No sir. Never did learn.
I learned to play at the war college. They taught us
the role of the bishop.
The bishop.
The Fighting bishop. Sword in one hand. Bible in

the other.

Well, sir, the MMPPs didn't have any bible.

You're our bishop, Sergeant. You and all the fighters with you. I can't tell you how important your forays are and what it means to every Armendrican. But I have one more question… If you'd read the signs before, would you have bought camping equipment and that scuba gear?

We didn't believe…

Believe? The time for Progs to believe ended on August 24th, Sergeant. Listen. I'm with you every time you go out there. Every drop of blood on that uniform you wear is a badge. Major Magat told us from the beginning what he was going to do.

The guys call him Flabby McFelon, Major.

Flabby McFelon…I like that.

Can I ask, sir, whose side are you on?

I don't get you, Sergeant.

You're blaming me? Blaming us? You know how many of us those pig-rutters slaughtered the first week of The Culling.

No. No, Sergeant. It's just that every day, with every encounter, I remember that Major Magat laid out what he was going to do to the courts. Not many of us listened. What he was going to do to Parlezment. What he was going to do to the country. To the army. To the social net. To us. He told us and some of us listened but we didn't understand that he wasn't normal and so we watched it happen—at the border, in the camps, in the cities and we said it wasn't so bad. Some of us said it didn't matter who sat in the Big Chair but it turns out it does matter and it's on us now to get back on beam. You know what I mean?

I do, Major.

Every time I send you out, I carry some of the guilt for ignoring what…what did you call him?

Flabby McFelon, Major.

For ignoring what Flabby McFelon said and has done, and I want you to know that somehow, sometime, we'll make it up to you and there will be…well…I don't know.

You're not to blame, Major. You were ready, but so many of us weren't.

Okay, Sergeant. Truck on over to the Armory for more gear and then go give those MMPPs a shot of hellfire for me.

One more thing, Major. You asked what I had in my closet on August 24th? Well, sure, I had camping equipment and scuba gear, but I also had a .223 and a .308 with a night scope, clips and a thousand rounds for each weapon. My sidearm is a Desert Eagle…

All legal, of course, Sergeant…

Most of it, Major…Well, some of it.

You were ready.

Kind of. I listened, sir. I heard them when they said it was a matter of time…

Flicker— the border Two Minor Magat Border Guards
MMBG 1 They gotta have water.
MMBG 2 They don't got no right to no water.
MMBG1 They die without water.
MMBG 2 Let 'em die. They's darkers. They's vermin.

Flicker—The desert. A Humvee. An explosion. Armendrican soldiers. The face of a soldier. Pock-marked and bleeding.

Flicker—on a knee. Torn. Bloody. A woman in uniform, eyes closed.

Flicker—Two bearded Magats carrying 15s shove a

blind-folded woman into a van. She wears a rainbow shirt, jeans, boots.

Flicker—a bleeding shoulder.

Flicker—One severed hand lies in the red dust of the Occupied Zone.

OPN

February. Year Two of the Culling

The Hall of Justice on Verguenza Avenue is a throw-back to innocent times when killing had a name and life had a meaning. The building is three stories of gray rusticated stone designed for a siege. The walls are thick. The doors steel with heavy bosses attached to the surface.

I enter by the side door, pass the Magat guard who averts his eyes when he looks at my mangled left hand—three fingers blown off in the jungle.

On the second floor, in front of a tribunal, a white woman wearing gray prison pantaloons and jerkin. On the jerkin, in yellow capitals

RACE TRAITOR

Head high, chin up, she stands defiant, hands at her sides.

She is barefoot.

Three Minor Magats poised at a table. They have the injured Magat collective demeanor—dead-eyed, self-righteous, entitled, puffed up pain.

Magat One, his name badge says Kevinouff. He wears the red robe of Magatian Jurisprudence.

You married a yellow skin.

You have no authority to hold me here.

Answer the question.

Show me your authority.

You see this? This is a 15. It's all the authority I need. Now answer the question. You married a yellow skin.

You know that or I wouldn't be here.

Yes or no?

I am here.

This yellowskin thinks he's a woman.

I am here.
He cut off his man parts.
I am here.
So what does that make him?
A better person than you.
You married a chink who thinks he's a woman?
He is not a chink.
Slant whatever. All the same. Thinks he's a woman.
She transitioned.
Transitioned. What does that mean?
You know what it means.
I know it makes you a lesbian.
I'm a human. I'm a woman.
Did you help this slant get away?
What do you think?
I think you'll find a place in a peelatorium.
You wretched excuse for a human being.

Magats prod the woman with their rifles. She spits at them. They laugh.

Kevinouff downs a shot of whiskey and then motion a Magat guard to bring in the next prisoner.

Flicker—A high rise in Laurentia looking over the Bay of Laurentia. Julia sits with her mother.
Armendrica is not a good place for you now.
Armendrica is not good for anybody right now.
And your children?
Dead? I don't know. I left before the Magats found me.

Flicker—A Magat palace in Seawenn. Opulence. Topiary Gardens. A flock of peacocks. Neo-Classical architecture. Glass. A dozen luxury vehicles—all from the Exterior.

DXM

I infiltrated the Seawenn Conference the week the Armendrican Alternative CCRC Housing Hedge Fund Manager worked out the market value of Blackskin versus Whiteskin and presented it to Lord Skum. Taking note, I stood behind Lord Skum at the conference table and heard the manager say,

Well, Lord Skum, pets just don't eat as much meat as people do. If you think about it and you want to monetize slaughter you don't want to waste all that meat under the blackskins.

Tell me more, youngish mon.

It's laid out in P 2025 that we push to monetize all aspects of production, transportation, agriculture, government, especially government so it's run like a corporation with one supreme power and one way to push that idea to its limits is to develop a mind-set that rewards corporations that capitalize death to enhance profits.

I like ze vay you sink, youngish mon, but don't ve already monetize death?

We do, Lord Skum, all that meat goes to waste when you bury it. But what would you think of a system that monetizes death beyond death?

Death beyond death? What is beyond death, youngish mon?

Suffering, Lord Skum. We know how to monetize death and we know how to monetize slaughter, but this idea, well, sir, it gives us a way to monetize suffering.

Monetize suffering? I zink you are onto somesing, youngish mon. Details?

Children, Lord Skum. We herd up all the brownskins, we pull the kids out and ship the parents to the peelatoria. That way the kids don't know who or what they are and the parents—well, you see? You take the next generation of brownskins back to zero and once the meat's

in cans, no one knows whale meat from steer meat
from…the haunch.

Ze haunch. Deliriously simple yet effective zinking youngish mon. But zis suffering? How do you put a dhaler value on such an ephemeral zing?

Flicker—Six huge black men—castrated, peeled, hanging from the I-5 overpass at Madison Street.
Flicker—A room full of crying children. They cuddle huddled together. They are chained at the wrists and ankles.
Flicker—Parlezment conference room. A panel of Blue Hats listens to a Brownskin woman.

June. Two Months Before the Culling

We were there that day Mister Master Magat Mueller Major Magat's head of policy and domestic carnage pitched Major Magat's proposition to Lord Skum to exterminate the Blackskins and all Brownskin Vermin and ease the strain on what remained of the social network by abolishing all taxes on the Pluts.

Well, Lord Skum, there's no money, per se, in blackskins, Mister Master Magat Mueller said, but with predictable domestic supply, there is a way to export the product to the entire international auto-industry including Teutonkria. You see, leather from livestock is both destructive and pernicious and depends on the demand for hamburgers in the North, whereas leather from an already fattened and existing supply, requires only a minimal infrastructure build-out, and a workforce committed to Major Magat's hegemoniacal dream.

Skins?

Hides, Lord Skum. Hides from a domestic well-fed source with a high fat content will give a better return than cow leather. Not only is it cheaper to produce, but there are no greenhouse gas emissions from the feedlots that are, in fact, already cutting into profits. And that all links to a reduced demand on the water supply. That is better for the political climate and, of course better for…us.

You mean ze.

Yes. Exactly MAWA.

Zo skins…uh hides from ze blackskins. And ze brown and yellow skins?

No cost up front…the stock is already well-fed and readily available.

And cheaper, you say.

Yes. If you ease the burden on the supply chain, the

end product sells at a high mark-up, and your profit margin goes astronomical.

Ah, ze famous Armendrican bargain. Make it cheap, sell it expensive.

Black tans well for purses and shoe leather.

Ach but ze international auto-industry does not use only bleck.

Of course not. Major Magat's plan includes a vast number of Whiteskins as well. Whiteskin, while slightly more expensive…

More expensive?

Harder to corral, libtard craziness, sir, but once in custody, the process is identical.

Und you don't mean ven you say Whiteskins us?

No. No. No. Not us. Libtards. Progs. Lefties. Comm-symps. Blue hats…

And how does zat happen?

They are, for the most part, unarmed.

Timetable?

Late spring, early summer. The Committee is still in process…

Back to ze hides, please.

A premium on the whiteskins for two reasons, Lord Skum. Whiteskins can be easily dyed to get exactly the shade the client wants. In fact, any shade the client wants but for blackskins the return is lower because they have to be bleached.

Pink? Purple? Brown?

Brown? That defeats the purpose, doesn't it? I mean natural leather. It will be a range from black through brown even yellow, but if you dye white skin black, what have you gained? The luxury demand for dyed leather is already enormous, and when we set the quotas, independent of the actual stockpile and or backlog, the profit margin for dyed white will still be exceptionally lucrative.

So you would dye white skin black?

We set supply, the market sets color and price. I recall that at one of Major Magat's rallies He said the sight of the brownskin vermin made him vomit but Major Magat doesn't see full potential in skin. His program is focused on killing the vermin who are poisoning our blood. But, of course, there is a minor problem with the progs.

And what might that be?

Bleeding hearts. Black Lives Matter. Me-Too. All that garbage is in the social discourse of cancel culture as of now, and there is no way to eradicate it without…I am reluctant to say it…a degree of *epidermal* cleansing.

Epidermal cleansing? Do you mean vat I sink you mean?

It's not what I want, of course, Lord Skum, but with the progs and libtards armed—which on Day One they don't seem to want—they are a problem for us if we proceed with the tanning….

Tanning? I thought zis would be simple…No middleman.

You don't want to eliminate the middleman completely, Lord Skum. That isn't the way the system works.

You sink I don't know how ze system works? Middleman always cuts into profits.

I apologize. Yes. Of course you know how the system works, that's why you have joined the other gentlemen here today. Of course tanning would cut into the profit margin even if we out-sourced it to the provinces or organizations in the Occupied Zones but that would involve shipping costs at a time when fuel is at a premium. Yes. No. Tanning will be a major part of the profit process with, as you say, the middleman extracting only the bare minimum from the pipeline. Of course, *Made in Armendrica* is the White…excuse me, right phrase. Each hide will come with that stamp to verify origin and authenticity. Something we can all be proud of.

You have no intention of outsourcing to ze Occupied Zones for supply zen?

Jobs for…well, you understand. Not in the foreseeable future. Domestic only, but if…well, if the plan matures properly, there is always a maybe, but until then this will be exclusively Armendrican skin.

I zee many maybes in there, youngish mon…

Major Magat has no intention of expanding beyond Armendrican borders, although I know that even you, Lord Skum, face some of the same issues that Major Magat has isolated here in Armendrica.

As you say, ze progs are a major problem for all of us.

No end to the easy money, Lord Skum.

I trust this won't be ze end of capitalism.

Of course not. As long as there is a pfennig to be made, there will be men of our ilk who will make it.

No matter ze social cost?

Was there ever a time when social cost was a factor in the equation, Lord Skum?

Ha! No limits. No controls. A perfect union.

Oh, Lord Skum. Don't, if you please, use *that* word!

One final issue, gentlemen. Meat disposal.

We have a White Paper on that, of course.

Und?

Pet food.

Pet food?

No cost for the product, no cost…well…of course for the herding, the gathering…some cost, but essentially it's free product.

When do we begin?

You give us the go-ahead and we won't even have to get Major Magat's scrawl in the EO. The machine is already in motion. We'll cull the big ones first.

The dangerous ones?

The big ones. The very big ones.

Flicker—Magats shooting their way into the Hawk weight room. The Hawks—big beefy men with angry eyes from time spent in the trenches working for their Capio owners—white men in tailor-made silk suits, rich white men who buy and sell and trade human flesh.

Flicker—The Prerugginian Ambassador meets Major Magat and his foreign minister-co-president of Master Magats after the Prerugginians reject a shipload of tanned hides.

Prerugginian Ambassador: Mister Major Magat, everything coming out of Armendrica is now past tense. No one, no one in Kukulkania, no one in Laurentia, not even in Kleisthenesia, no one wants anything with the name Armendrica stamped on it. Made in Armendrica is now a sign of genocide, Mister Major Magat.

Major Magat: Would you be saying, uh, that…my…oh, shit, fuck, that even you, you scum Peruginagians even with all your fucking fucked up fucking shit talk Armendrican.

Flicker—a freighter entering Prerugginian Harbor stopped by OBUP Coastal Control.

As Coastal Control boards the freighter port-side, Magats dump flats of tanned Blackskin to starboard.

Pyotr Xian Johnson: It's *Prerugginians*, and she is speaking Armendrican, Mister Major Magat.

Major Magat: It doesn't sound like she's speaking Armendrican.

Pyotr Xian Johnson: She is speaking Armendrican, Mister Major Magot. She has an accent.

Major Magat: A defective, then. Who let this pan-suited pussy in anyway?

Pyotr Xian Johnson: You did, Mister Major Magat, sir.

Major Magat: What does she want? All the Brownies want something. What?

Pyotr Xian Johnson: It's about product, Mister Major Magat. Rotting product.

Prerugginian Ambassador: Yes, Major Magat, rotting product.

Major Magat: What is this some kind of perrispal for a few blackskins.

Pyotr Xian Johnson: More than a few, Major Magat.

Major Magat: Who is this again?

Pyotr Xian Johnson: The Prerugginian Ambassador, Major Magat.

Major Magat: Prerugginian? Where the hell is Preruginiaga and why is she here? Do I owe her money?

Pyotr Xian Johnson: Before the Culling, Mister Major Magat, Prerugginia was a major trading partner, but when the skinning and the peeling went industrial and you EOed the exportation of the product there were lapses in the quality control and tons of second-rate skins went out and the Ambassador is here to try to make it right.

Major Magat: So I don't owe her money.

Pyotr Xian Johnson: No. No money. Skins. Blackskins. Tanned blackskins. They rejected the shipment.

Major Magat: Who rejected the shipment? What kind of asshole are you?

Pyotr Xian Johnson: I'm your foreign minister, Mister Major Magat. Pyotr Xian Johnson. And the facts are that not even the Prerugginians will buy our products.

Major Magat: There has to be alternative facts, Jensen.

Pyotr Xian Johnson: Not in this case, Mister Major Magat. The facts are plain and simple.

Flicker—Harbor Warehouse in Prerugginia. Stacks of Blackskins rotting maggot filled. Flies streaming off the stacks of Blackskins. Prerugginians wearing gasmasks using front loaders pile the rotting stacks of Blackskins onto semis.

Major Magat: Used to count on the Paraginagnians before the libtard-commie-Fascist-Porgressives cut the shit out our policy and poisoned our blood.

Pyotr Xian Johnson: Prerugginians, Mister Major Magat, not Paraginagnians.

Major Magat: Who the hell are we talking to right now…what is your name?

Pyotr Xian Johnson: Johnson. Pyotr Xian Johnson.

Major Magat: And what's the problem?

Pyotr Xian Johnson: The problem, Mister Major Magat, is that it was bad policy merging White Christian Nationalist religion with Capitalism.

Major Magat: Your name is Xian, so what the fuck is the matter?

Prerugginian Ambassador: Mister Magat Major…

Major Magat: Major Magat, woman. Major…then Magat.

Prerugginian Ambassador: When you crossed White Christian Nationalism with Capitalism, it was a very bad decision because, we, the Prerugginians, are not White Christian Nationalists and we now know that the Blackskins you sent us are not dyed buffalo skins at all as the trade agreement said they would be. They are Blackskins tanned and not well tanned and they are rotting and our auto industry is on the verge of collapse because when the Alliance of Trading Nations discovered that Armendrica has cheated and was sending us tanned animal hides for use in our industry, they boycotted our products and refuse to honor the Trade Agreement by refusing to export their animal hides to Prerugginia.

Major Magat: What the holy fuck is going on here?

Pyotr Xian Johnson: What she's saying is that when you made Armendrica White, and when you deported all the brownskins, it was a mistake because when the Pride started skinning the blacks, she asks, how did you expect any nation left on the planet to buy what you make?

Major Magat: What I make? I don't understand a god-damned word this pussy is saying, Jones

Pyotr Xian Johnson: Johnson, Mister Major Magat, Johnson. Pyotr Xian Johnson. And when I say *what you make*, Mister Major Magat, I don't mean that you, Major Magat, actually make it. I mean that the capitalist combine that bought you the office that made the trade agreement, as you can now see, is a disaster because to put it bluntly, Mister Major Magat, they fucked up by selling human skin as ersatz animal skin. Now no one will buy a thing they make so it's not just the skins they are boycotting, but any and everything made in Armendrica and that is destroying the Prerugginian automotive industry and by extension the boycott of all things not only Armendrican but also Prerugginian.

Major Magat: So this rotting skin thing is my fault? What kind of idiot do you think I am, Jensen?

Pyotr Xian Johnson: It's Johnson. Pyotr Xian Johnson.

Major Magat: You better get your ass in gear and do something about this mess you've created, Jenkins.

Pyotr Xian Johnson: It's Johnson, Pyotr Xian Johnson.

Prerugginian Ambassador: There is one more matter…

Major Magat: Who is this piece of shit pussy interrupting me, Jones?

Prerugginian Ambassador: I am the Prerugginian Ambassador and I have a brief from my government…

Major Magat: Government? I thought that Medved

and me got rid of all government bullshit…

Pyotr Xian Johnson: Only in Armendrica, Mister Major Magat.

Major Magat: What? We didn't get it all?

Pyotr Xian Johnson: I'm sure I'm not the first Armendrican to tell you this sir, Mister Major Magat, but the world is bigger than Armendrica.

Prerugginian Ambassador: My brief, Mister Major Magat, in my brief there is also the matter of meat.

Flicker—A dock in Prerugginia. A ship unloading pallets marked with Meat Ready to Eat. Product of Armendrica.

Major Magat: Meat? What meat?

Prerugginian Ambassador: Tons of it, Mister Major Magat. Ship loads of meat that your people in the trade agreement assured us would be for pets, but what arrived was, in fact, canned and labeled as Ready to Eat meat for Humans (low veg content).

Major Magat: Arrest this woman.

Flicker—A restaurant in Prerugginia. Dozens of Prerugginians vomiting, on the floor, writhing. EMTs working the sick. White body bags lined up.

Pyotr Xian Johnson: Uh, we can't do that, Major Magat.

Major Magat: I am the Prince and the Pride here and if I say arrest this speaker, you will arrest them.

Pyotr Xian Johnson: You can't arrest her because Armendrica has diplomatic relations secured by mutual agreements which means you can't lay a hand on her or it invalidates the Trade Agreement and that won't set well with the Pluts whose pockets you have your hands in and they in yours, Mister Major Magat.

Major Magat: Well fuck that diplomatic shit, I'll do what I want. I am the law. I am the Holy God.

Prerugginian Ambassador: The meat, Mister Major Magat. The meat. It made our people sick.

Major Magat: Sick? Well take it up with the…What's it called, Jensen?

Pyotr Xian Johnson: The G F and M A and it's *J O H N S O N*. Johnson

Major Magat: Well, fuck them, Jones, take it up with the GF and MA.

Pyotr Xian Johnson: The Prerugginians can't do that, Mister Major Magat, because the GF and MA is no more.

Major Magat: No more GF and MA? What the hell is GF and MA, anyway?

Pyotr Xian Johnson: You and Lord Skum abolished the Good Food and Medicine Administration two years ago and subsumed it into the T S and P D.

Major Magat: Then take it up with the TS and PD, Jones.

Pyotr Xian Johnson: There is only one manager at TS and PD, Mister Major Magat, and Lord Skum furloughed her and all her staff and privatized all the data.

Flicker—The Prerugginian Ambassador in the office of the President of Prerugginia handing the President a document.

The Prerugginian Ambassador opens her briefcase. She hands a document to Pyotr Xian Johnson who hands it to Major Magat.

Major Magat: And what is this?

Prerugginian Ambassador: Read it, Mister Major Magat.

Pyotr Xian Johnson: He doesn't read…long documents, Ambassador, can you summarize?

Pyotr scans the document.
Pyotr Xian Johnson: Holy shit.

*Flicker—The Office of the President of Prerugginia.
A dozen ministers from all of OBUP sign a document then
give the document to the Prerugginian Ambassador who
tucks the document in to her briefcase.*

Pyotr looks at the Ambassador, brow wrinkled,
mouth open. He hands the document to Major Magat as the
Ambassador exits the office.
Major Magat: What does it say and why is that bitch
turning her back on me?
Pyotr Xian Johnson: Prerugginia is unilaterally
withdrawing from the OBUP Trade Agreement, Mister
Major Magat, and it's not just because of the rotting skins.
The Prerugginian government has written, "We will not eat
human meat."
Major Magat: Unaliterally withdrawing? What the
holy crap! I'm the only one who can do that, Pyotr X.
Jensen. I'm the only living god on this earth…well…
Medved and me, we are the only living gods on this earth
and they better get the lead out of their asses or there will
be hellfire and nukes up their asses.

*Flicker—At the Laurentian border a flood of red-
capped Armendricans stopped at the border. Long lines of
cars, tops piled with gear. Red caps, bills turned so the
MAWA shows only from behind.*

*Flicker—At the Kukulkanian border, guards armed
in riot gear—helmets, masks, gloves, armor- plated vests—
hold back red-capped Armendricans storming the
barricades.*

Flicker—At a Laurentian immigrant camp, just

*outside the border, Armendricans huddled in tents, cold.
Empty cans of meat Ready to Eat piled outside each tent.*

*Flicker—A Kukulkanian immigrant camp enclosed
with barbed, electrified wire. Armendricans living in their
cars. Each Armendrican wears a Red Arm Patch stitched
with Illegal Alien in heavy black thread.*

DXM

The empire is lost in the marches. No one knows
what that means now that history is banned in Armendrica.
The Romanisch knew the truth—often building their
strongest barriers at the borders—so I learned in history,
before the Magats abolished the study of all pre-white
Christianity and burned all the books in all the libraries in
Armendrica. With the burning of books, they forbade
anyone to import books, and that left Armendrica, a
country between Kukulkania and Laurentia, in the grip of a
growing ignorance, sprinkled with spots of conspiracy
theories about everything from the origin of the universe to
natural selection and vegetables.

In the early days, there were secretive study units—
taught by women—spread through the Cities, but as
Magatism wormed its way into the minds and brains of
Armendricans, the Magats attacked the Clandestine
Schools and burned their books, exiled or murdered the
teacher-ones, the ones with knowledge of the past and that
forced learning deeper underground. When the Magats
abolished all history that left so few with a memory of the
time when we learned about the past and in learning about
the past, learned how to correct our mistakes. The Magats,
until the Progs took control of the ammunition factories,
had only one item in their agenda—Kill all Darkskinned
people. When that failed, when the Progs and the Libtards
and the Lefties took control, the Minor Magats preached

their lost cause to fewer and fewer and in the end of the Culling, few left in Armendrica flew their Magat flags, but took them in, folded them, stored them and avowed forever allegiance to democracy and freedom speech.

So few have now even an inkling of the past and I am one of them.

Prerugginia to the East.

Pariggia to the West.

Kukulkania to the South.

Laurentia to the North.

I stand here at the border of Laurentia watching the Armendrican immies crowded into barbwire holding camps on the Laurentian side. Camps that are filthy, insect-infested, thick with filth that Armendricans never imagined living in, but there they are—exiles who fled at the Apex of the Culling when the Progs had seized control of half of Armendrica, half the cities in Armendrica, half the neighborhoods in that half of Armendrica, and the Minor Magats—vowing never to give up their weapons, vowing either to kill all Progs, Libtards, and Lefties, or leave the country—had left and there they are trapped at the borders, in camps that the Laurentians built to contain them rather than let them enter Laurentia as illegals. Illegals because there was no central government in charge of protocols, there were no visas, no exit visas, no timbres because government had ceased to exist, and the Laurentians will not let the exiles into Laurentia. There is a joke going around in the Laurentian capital—*tell them to leave their guns at the border.*

In the camps, I hear Minor Magats still fighting for their lost cause, still plotting the murder of hundreds of thousands just as they had murdered and skinned people in the early days of the Culling.

Minor Magat 1—We gotta identify every libtard lyer. Make every one of them suicide right in front of a million armed men. We gotta go to Armendrica City and hang every Prog in the fake Parlezment. That's the only way to make them pay for their treasonness.

Minor Magat 2—This country is out of control. When we get it back we'll kill all of'em we missed the first time.

Minor Magat 3—I hope every lefty dies 'cause they gots to pay for what they done.

Minor Magat 4—May the Holy God strike them all dead. We remember J6 and they gonna pay!

White Immies without a home. White Immies with nothing but their impotent and empty AR 15s—gutted and useless without ammunition. White Immies with no egress, no future, no money, no food except through the largesse of the Laurentians who were not hesitant to feed the hungry, to medicate the sick, but were not ready to allow overt secessionist troublemakers into Laurentia because Laurentia had fought its own battles with secession and Laurentians know that Magatism is an infectious disease that destroys parts of the brain.

After they had exhausted their hoards of stocked supplies, the exiled Minor Magats, the preppers as they once called themselves, relied on the canned meat Ready to Eat that the Laurentian managers had confiscated and stored in warehouses at the border where in the latter days of the Culling, they had quarantined them as food not fit for human beings.

To the South, the situation was identical—warehouses, at each border crossing—stacks and stacks of crates full of canned meat Ready to Eat handed out to the Minor Magats—their wives, their children, their nephews and nieces—who gorged on the meat and declared that it tasted good but could use a bit of salt.

At the southern crossing, the problem was double and troubling.

The Kukulkanian border guards had tangled with

the Magats since the first Major Magat presidency and
now, with the collapse of government and the withdrawal
of the border agency, the Kukulkanians armed the fences
not to keep Southern immies out of Armendrica but to keep
the Armendrican escapees in. Squeezed by their own
malfeasance, the Migrant Minor Magats—on both North
and South borders—were eating nothing but their own
bitterness because of the shortage of bread.

DXM

January 6th First Year of the Culling

I shadow him as Major Magat enters the rally in a
shaft of light that tracks his way through the throng of
hand-picked acolytes gathered on the dais.

With each step, the deplorables chant—
Make
>> Armendrica
>>> White
>>>> Again
Make
>> Armendrica
>>> Great
>>>> Again

And with each step Major Magat raises his clenched
fist in the salute that is now his personal sign of Oneness
with the crowd.

He stands at the podium in a shaft of golden light
that reflects off his bronzed face turning it into a metallic
mask.

He shoots his fist into the air again and the
deplorables chant and with each pump of his fist the
women in the throng take out bottles of perfume,
disinfectant, air spray, some of them reach into sack purses
to pull out hair spray and still the deplorables—held at a
distance from the Perfect One—chant Major Magat Major
Magat.

So, Wormbrain, right, everybody likes Wormbrain.
And he's so big into the health, food, and women, things,
everything, he wants to do things—and the environment.
And he endorsed me, the first time a Wormbrain has ever
endorsed a Magat and maybe it's going to be the last, but I
doubt it. And he's a great guy. Wormbrain.

He would be so perfect but that would make him

more perfect than I am and I'm perfect so he doesn't like artificial foods, and he doesn't like pesticides and all the stuff they put on him. And if you listen to him for ten minutes, I mean, he says, "Other countries that don't do anything are healthier than us, OK?" We're not that healthy—To put it mildly. So, no artificial foods. We don't want artificial— we have plenty of food. The food isn't our problem. And our farmers are great, and our farmers aren't allowed to do their job. You know our farmers did great. Four years ago, they were doing the—just about the best they've ever done.

They're not doing well at all now. We're not going to have artificial foods. We don't want artificial foods, we want healthy foods. And a lot of things are going to be going. And I'll tell you, I'm going to have Wormbrain involved in it. He's a great guy. And even the way—when I mentioned his name, all of you guys—and you're tough cookies.

You know, you wouldn't think sometimes, you'd say, maybe you wouldn't like a guy like Bobby. But he—he's a person that talks more about food and health than anything else. So I think that's cool. So, we'll get it—we'll get it taken care of. So, what is he going to do to increase organic foods in urban communities? You ask him You ask Wormbrain and he'll tell you.

And then I notice the clothes pins.

Dozens of them. Hundreds of them clamped over the nostrils of each obedient nose of the Perfect One as he passes and then, just as Major Magat, the Perfect One speaks, a young woman, holding a golden cross tight to her chest, loses her clothespin and she gasps and faints and falls to the floor but no one stoops to help her to her feet and Major Magat shouts into the microphone—I am the greatest president that Armendrica has ever had and we have accom—cumm—com com plished more than any Armendrican president in history.

And he waits as the Minor Magats chant…
White Choice
The Only Choice
Down with Brown
We are White
We are Christian
Your Rules Don't Apply to Us

Flicker—A ROM dead of a heart attack lying naked on a young Black woman who inspects her bright red fingernails then rolls the ROM off.

DXM

May. One Year Before the Culling

I am in the pharmacy on Proclamation Boulevard when a ROM enters. He looks angry, but it is hard not to notice that all Magats look angry, so I go back to shopping. The shelves are near-bare, but the prices are near-peak. I hear the ROM shout as though he is the only person in the pharmacy.

ROM—I don't get it. Why can't I get it?

ProgPhar—You sent a woman.

ROM—Yeah. She's my wife.

ProgPhar—Major Magat doesn't recognize women and she doesn't have your name, sir and only you can get the prescription.

ROM—So I had to come.

ProgPhar—That's the rule.

ROM—Who makes the rule?

ProgPhar—The rule-making board.

ROM—Who's on that board?

ProgPhar—The rule-making board is made up of licensed MDs, licensed Pharmacists, licensed Medical researchers and board certified attorneys at law.

ROM—All progs.

ProgPhar—All Progs.

ROM—All educated, hi-falutin' college-educated progs. Oughta shut down those educational institutions…

ProgPhar—If you mean the colleges and universities, Major Magat's already working on that with the defunding and the student loan interest increases and the book burning, and the…

ROM—You one of those educated idiots?

ProgPhar—I am a pharmacist, sir. Only one of three women pharmacists in Armendrica. To be a pharmacist, you need a degree and then another degree and then board certification but I don't own this pharmacy because I finished my education so deep in debt I can never own it.

ROM—How much?

ProgPhar—Three-hundred thousand Armendrican…

ROM—Three hundred thousand. Jesus fucking bald-headed christ.

ProgPhar—Three hundred thousand is nothing compared to what it costs AMM2.

ROM—No no no. How much do you want to double that prescription?

ProgPhar—You mean how much would you have to pay me?

ROM—That's right.

ProgPhar—You're on the Safety Net, sir, so you don't have to pay me, you do have to co-pay for the prescription and for that I'll need a credit card.

ROM—I need more than one.

ProgPhar—More than one card?

ROM—Pill. Double it.

ProgPhar—Uh, it's a regulated drug, sir, so the limit is one per month.

ROM—Regulated. When did that start?

ProgPhar—AMM 2 Parlezment enacted a consumer protection protocol during the last administration.

ROM—AMM 2? What does that mean?

ProgPhar—After Major Magat 2.

ROM—Do you know who I am?

ProgPhar—Your name is on the prescription, so yes, I know who you are.

ROM—All progs in that Parlezment…

ProgPhar—Uh, I don't know, I mean I think there are Master Magats and a few Minor Magats in Parlezment as well, that's why they can't get anything done except the takeaways.

ROM—Takeaways? What do you mean,

takeaways?

ProgPhar—They take away your safety net and that's why your prescription costs you so much. Then they take away everything else and what does that leave?

ROM—But all those progs in Parlezment control everything, don't they?

ProgPhar—Not everything, sir.

ROM—How much?

ProgPhar—Sir…

ROM—I mean how much do I owe you?

ProgPhar—For one unit? Ten thousand Armendrican.

ROM—Ten thousand? For one pill? Didn't used to be that much.

ProgPhar—Yes that was BMM 1, sir. As I said sir, Mycoxaflopin is a regulated drug and it is very powerful and it's expensive because the MJs did an historical review and decided that there's nothing in the books that lets the Parlezment set or control anything so it's do whatever you want whenever you want and that's how Big Pharma prices it and there's nothing I or you can do about it. That's why the trains don't run on time, too. So, pay up or keep it zipped up.

ROM—I guess I been hiding out, 'cause what you're telling me is that things aren't what they were before Major Magat sold the government.

ProgPhar—You understand, sir, that once the MJs make decisions without logic and relying only on history they can do anything they want and we don't have any say in what they are going to do.

ROM—How do you know all this if you're just a ProgPhar?

ProgPhar glances around the pharmacy, leans into the ROM. She whispers, 'I went to school, sir, and I read books because I hid my library from the Minor Magats when the book burning began.'

ROM—You read books?

ProgPhar—That will be ten thousand, sir.

ROM—Gotta tell you, that's a lotta cash for one fuck. Wait…You read books?

ProgPhar—Yes, sir. It is a lot of cash but think about how many ways Major Magot is fucking you every day in every way.

ROM—If I want to die in the saddle, that's a horse I'm gonna ride and they don't got no business tellin' me what to do tween the sheets.

ProgPhar—That's right, sir, but they, and you know who I mean, don't have any trouble making sure a woman can't control her own body…

ROM—What do you mean they?

ProgPhar—They. You know. The Magats who want to make it expensive so whoever you're rocking and rolling with, the chances you'll sprout a junior is high if the price is out of this world.

ROM—Well fuck them whoever they are.

ProgPhar—That's the Magat's new natalist policy—the more mouths there are to feed the higher the profit for the agri-business conglomerates and the more souls there are for the Xters to pray into heaven for when the rapture comes and the more Magats there are to vote the Master Magats and Minor Magats into Parlezment.

ROM—What the fuck are you talking about?

ProgPhar—Just laying out for you the consequences of conflating capitalism, white Christian nationalism and magat politics and pushing religious legislation that has only one goal and that is to take away your freedom of choice—they win, you lose, Old Man.

ROM—That's just plain fucking crazy. Who are they?

ProgPhar—Of course they're saying, as you say, you can fuck all you want, whoever you want, but if it bears fruit they don't want you plucking it before it's ripe.

ROM—You lost me there, little lady.

ProgPhar—How did you vote last election, Old Man?

ROM—Went red, of course 'cause that's the way the vulpine shows called it.

ProgPhar—Well, that's who you voted for, Pops. Good luck getting into Laurentia if you want a boner before your month is up.

ROM—You're talking some pretty strong anti-shit here, Miss ProgPhar.

ProgPhar—Yes sir, but this is the only pharmacy in Pharville with any Mycoxaflopin in stock and you're not my only customer. You know you could buy the drug from the Prerugginians or the Laurentians and it wouldn't cost you anything, but you'd have to go North or purchase it online and the MJs have out-lawed the internet in Armendrica.

ROM—Well I'll tell you this, Armendrica ain't what it was before Major Magat got bought.

ProgPhar—Alternatively you can go to Kleisthenesia or Kukulkania or Laurentia where they sell the drug for less than we do here in Armendrica City and if you're on their safety net it's free but they won't let you into their country so you'd have to take the bus but the buses don't run on time because the MJs banned out-of-state travel unless you're a Plut.

ROM—What do you mean it's free? The MJs? You mean the MJs.

ProgPhar—Did I say free?

ROM—You said free in Prerugginia.

ProgPhar—Well, just as it used to be in Armendrica BMM 1.

ROM—How much?

ProgPhar—The problem is the conflict between the politics and the church and between the church and the capitalists.

ROM—Just fill the prescription. Okay?
ROM pulls a credit card from his wallet.

I follow the ROM from the pharmacy and into an apartment building on Judgment Avenue. There is a sign still on the building
THE SHIELD
Elder Care-Memory Care
Assisted Living at its Finest.

It is a six-story brick and glass structure. On the sixth floor, the ROM enters apartment 621. I enter behind him. He doesn't see me, hear me, feel me, smell me. I listen as he talks to the woman—she is Black. She is twenty. Stocky. Hennaed hair. The ROM says,
Gonna cost us an arm and a leg to get it on now, babe. You won't believe what I just learned.
It's always something, sugar, but as long as you got it, we can get it on okay.
I ain't sure we did the right thing voting MAWA.
I didn't vote MAWA, hon.
You ready?
I'm always ready to haul your ashes, sugar. Come and eat lunch.

Flicker—A naked ROM on a bed...dead. Beside him a young black woman with hennaed hair polishes her nails.

Flicker—A train running at full speed onto a high trestle bridge. When the train reaches half-way, the bridge collapses. The train drops into the river.

Flicker—A dam on a river. A roaring, the dam breaks, water shoots through the widening cracks. A wall of water gushes downstream towards a small city.

Flicker—A town, at night, the roar of water hitting houses. Tall buildings topple.

Flicker—EMTs in their ambulances and fire trucks swept away by the wall of water.

November 26th First Year of the Culling

He enters the press room through a side door.

I follow.

Immense quiet over the room.

Reporters—red caps, laptops—sit hunched like stone gargoyles carved.

He stands at the podium.

He wears a Blackskin Cape over his royal blue suit. White shirt and yellow tie.

The cape clasps at the neck.

He flaps his arms, the cape flies opens. The skin of his face that ash-gray.

I wait. I know he can't see me, won't see me because like all Magats he sees only what he wants to see. Hears only what he wants to hear. And, as a writer, a digger, a truth-seeker in Thanatopia, I have to hide—in disguise, a dozen ways to dress, inserts in my shoes to make me taller, a knee brace to keep from dragging my wounded foot

He leans into the microphone. He says, You don't have to do anything except sit there and look pretty 'cause I'll ask and answer all my questions.

The reporters—all men except for two women who sit legs crossed in full view of the podium—laugh that nervous laugh they spew when Major Magat opens his mouth and repeats the same thing he said last time they forced themselves into prisoner mode and sat in fake intensity, leaning forward to catch the tall woman joke, the poison immigrant-rapist-murderer-job-stealer joke, the anti-Libtard rant that always gouged a nervous giggle from the mixed blood reporters who had sold their honor and their past just to sit in the room with the Perfect One—knowing as they sat that if the PO suspected black or brown blood in any face, Minor Magats would peel that face down to the bone and from the epidermal covering of the body cut out another Black Cape that another Minor Magat would sell to another angry, violent White Dude to wear as a cloak and sigil of White Supremacy just as the Perfect One was wearing it—preening before the mixed blood reporters who knew without knowing that someone's mother, father uncle, aunt, grandmother, sister, brother and been peeled down to white bone in a peelatorium then boiled to broth and turned into meat Ready to Eat or its half-sister, Pet Food—Not For Human Consumption.

I know this.

I have been inside the peelatorium on Sanctimony Promenade. Smelled the blood, seen the skin slit off at the hands of Minor Magats—'doing their job, doing that the Master Magats told them to do'—then watched the tanners work the hides into leather that went, when tanned, to the stylists and the merchants for sale to the Pluts who wore their leftie, colored, Brownskinned, Blackskinned enemies and without a catch in their throats flaunted their power…And the reporters, the press asked no questions of the Perfect One because his answers were always the same answers to the same questions he asked himself—Who are the immigrants, the criminals streaming across our borders coming to rape and murder that tall woman who voted for me and steal your job?

I watch Major Magat at the podium declare that he has no idea who the miscreaturants—he always stumbles over the three syllable words—who wrote P 2025, no idea who signed it because he didn't know anything about it.

He shrugs. His black cape folds again over his white shirt and yellow tie and he disappears in the blackness— except for the orange mane and the bronzed skin metallized to make him look like a god-statue and, he says he doesn't know anything about what's happening at the border because he has people who take care of that and the

children are brown so no one bothers with them besides it's
a lie anyway all of it is a lie, fake news, and it gives him a
timetable that a relatable informer told him that
Peruffin…Previr… Preuviriniangia…is with—hold—ing-
draw-ing from the OBPU trade agreement which is fine
with him because who needs a bunch of leftie socialist
lying foreigners anyway and then a reporter, one of the
women, stands and the Perfect One's jaw drops in anger,
frustration, disbelief that a woman would interrupt him
when he is in the middle of an important and necessary
announcement about white men. The woman says,

Mister Major Magat, sir, why are the Prerugginians
withdrawing from the OBPU trade agreement?

Major Magat says,

They're all lefties, Progs, Immies, Antis, that's why.

But Sir, Mister Major Magat, what will that do to
the GNP?

The what?

The GNP, Mister Major Magat.

Mister Major Magat swivels, looks at the curtain,
mouth open, palms up in disbelief, and says,

What hell is the GNP, anyway?

Balding, tight-lipped Mister Master Magat Mueller
wearing a gray pinstriped suit and a red tie with white
polka dots steps through the opening in the curtain and
walks to Major Magat, the Perfect One. He points at the
woman who asked the question. He says,

Who are you?

I'm a reporter Mister Mueller Magat, sir, just a
reporter.

Reporters are out-lawed so what are you a woman
doing asking questions of Major Magat? You know he asks
the questions and answers only the ones he wants to answer
so shut your bitch female mouth and sit down.

I beg to differ Mister Master Mueller Magat, sir, but
Major Magat outlawed journalists not reporters, Mister

Master Mueller Magat sir. I am a reporter.

Right. So what is your question for Major Magat?

Why is Mister Major Magat wearing a Blackskin cape if he knows nothing about P 2025? Mister Master Magat Mueller?

Mister Master Magat Mueller whispers into Major Magat's ear and the Perfect One nods and Mister Master Magat Mueller points at the questionetter and says,

Arrest this leftie-symp and haul her female ass to the closest peelatorium.

From the back ranks of the press, the four huge bearded burly big-bellied Minor Magats emerge. Giants wearing Pendleton Plaid Shirts, camo fatigues, combat boots, and carrying AR 15s snatch the questionetter up and, hands under her skirt, grabbing, more than likely, her pussy, the big bellied bearded burlies drag her out of the press room. She kicks and screams until one of the burlies jams a rag into her mouth.

Major Magat waves his hand at the press corps. He says,

Any other questions out there that I won't answer.

A timid little man wearing pince nez glasses raises his hand. Mister Master Magat Miller points at him. The little man says,

Is the Blackskin cape why the Prerugginians are voiding the trade agreement?

Later, in the peelatorium on Sanctimony Promenade I watch a peeler string up the questionetter by her Achilles tendons, head down, gagged, and disembowel her with a single swipe of a flensing knife and with a deftness I've not seen before, peel her, split her, quarter her, and butcher her. In the silence of that death, the four burly bearded big-bellied giants stare at the stacks of meat the butcher drops on the conveyor as it carries the meat through the portal to the cooker.

Gone then the meat, the Minor Magats exit the peelatorium. Faces placid. AR 15 s strung across their burly bodies. One of them jostles another. He says,
Whadya say to a cold one?

DXM

A woman stands. She is dressed in blue—blue blouse, blue slacks, blue stockings, blue pumps laced with blue bows. Adding to the chant, she calls out, and the Culling, Major Magat? What about the Culling? And Major Magat shouts that Mister Master Magat Mueller has people handling that…Culling at the border and our exports to Prerugginia and the tall woman who voted for me products from Armendrica and the Woman in Blue shouts,

No one will buy your stinking products made in Armendrica, Major Magat, no one wants you or anything made in your Armendrica anymore.

A sudden silence then, I hear clothespins dropping to the floor of the dais and I see women holding handkerchiefs over their faces as they turn their backs on Major Magat and his monster-maker Mister Master Magat Mueller and as the auditorium empties I see Major Magat standing alone at the podium and he looks out over the emptiness strewn with ripped placards and there in the center of the auditorium I see the Woman in Blue and I am she and she holds up a sign emblazoned with three words in bright blue—

YOU ARE IRRELEVANT

Flicker— In a Mountain Palace, four silk-suited Pluts, whose annual bonuses exceed the entire payroll of the entire workforce under each of them, sit around a table—could be the same table they sat at the Seawenn Conference. They peel the bank bands off bundles of dhalers and then toss the bundles into a fire box at the end of the table.

August 24th Year Four of the Culling

Plut 1: I had a dream the other night. Made me think. This prog had me chained to a table and he had my thumb in a vise and he kept twisting it and with each twist he said, you realize that your monetary policies have turned you into prey? And I said, well, turnabout is fair play. And then you know what happened? A dozen progs chained all of us, you, me—yes all of us—up and they strapped each and every one of us down on the ground—Jesus God it was cold, you know—and the prog said take off your silk suit because you won't need them where you're going. The poor will trap you, boil you then eat you.

Plut 2: How much did you take in AMM2?

Plut 1: In Armendrican dhalers?

Plut 2: Any currency.

Plut 1: Pre-tax?

Plut 2: You paid taxes?

Plut 1: You're funny. Of course, you know I didn't pay taxes.

Plut 3: I never paid taxes. Anybody who paid taxes under Master Magat was either a fool or a prog.

Plut 2: Is there a difference?

Plut 4: Listen. Do you hear something? I hear something. Listen.

Plut 1: Probably the progs coming to castrate you and make you eat your own nuts.

September. Year Four of the Culling

Heard the progs nabbed Major Magat.

Yeah. Charged him with eating people.

People? I heard it was blackskins he took the hit for.

And I heard the progs who got him was blackskins.

Blackskins can't arrest Major Magat.

Lay you bitcoin to dog turds and hold the stakes in my mouth they arrested him and …

Enough. Enough.

…boil him.

I hear they boiled a hundred hedge fund managers in Kleisthenesia.

All you've got left is conspiracy theories…Let it go.

Let it go? You'll see when they come for us and peel and boil us…

They won't boil us, you soundin' like a prog, m'man.

You know they will boil you. Strip you, cut you, castrate you—all of us—boil us. Then eat us. We've driven them that low.

Yeah. Look what your conspiracy theories got us, asshole.

How do you know they're just theories?

Name one, just one that panned out.

Yeah, you're right. Didn't work out for us. Wait. What if we re-dye the Whiteskins? Get exactly the shade you want.

Don't you understand what has happened, man? The progs have kicked our asses. Made in Armendrica is a stigma, a scab, a scar on the planet. Made in Armendrica is a sign of decay and misdirection.

That's not true. We can still supply the transportation industry with quality material—unique, you know, and unique really sells to the niche markets with the right incentive. I see huge discounts, great ads, you know—

Get it here, Real Armendrican Leather. Leather so soft you can feel it breathe…

Too late.

But listen—maybe we went the wrong way on the skins. You know? When I say purse what do you think? Every Magatte needs a purse, right? And not just one—You see? That's the kicker—I can see pink, red, black…maybe not black, yellow…uh…maybe not yellow, but shades of red and hues of pink and clutches, you know, for those luxury evenings you spend with your hubby. So we launch a new line and we call the scheme The Right Purse for the Right Woman. Brilliant! Right?

Hey, man, come on. Listen to yourself. No one will buy anything with the name Armendrica stamped on it and it don't matter if it's leather car seats or clutches or sack purses 'cause made in Armendrica is a sign of genocide.

You hungry? Maybe we can eat the evidence. LMAO.

You're not listening. Not even the Prerugginians will buy from us. Could always count on the Prerugginians. Anything made in Armendrica they ate up. Ya know. Not now. Your conspiracy theories? You want the truth?

Are you sure we can't just rebrand all the pet food…

You repackage crap and call it candy but it's still crap so what does it get us? The libtards got it right. You don't cross White Nationalist Religion with Capitalism.

All this product rotting. There's got to be a way to make money out of rot.

What the hell! You haven't heard one word I've just told you. It's the end.

Why all this reprisal? So some of us knocked off a few Blacks. They breed like flies on a corpse, so why get all worked up about it?

You and Major Magat and all his Master Magats and Minor Magats, you made Armendrica white again and you still want the rest of the planet to buy what we make? Get it through your skull—the rest of the world ain't white. You cross politics and white religion and capitalism and you get your Thanatopia but then what?

Do I detect a pinch of revisionism coming out of your mouth?

The only revisionism possible is to know and understand the truth of what we…yes…we have done.

It is. By the holy god, it is revisionism oozing between those teeth.

Adapt or they will eat you.

Who's going to eat me?

Look around you.

So, really, all you're saying is it's the end of the easy money.

That's what I'm saying. If they let you live, you might have to work for it now.

End of bonuses. End of capitalism.

You still don't see what has happened.

Major Magat said it was good business.

Feeding people-burgers to other people and selling people-hides to car manufacturers wasn't the best idea that ever came out of the hedge-fund mind.

People-hides? Holy God. You know, when you say it like that, it has a fine ring…You know what we can do? We can deny it. Right? We didn't, well, you know, personally have anything to do with it, and I didn't, you know it, I didn't vote for Major Magat Seashol. No one I know voted for them and that bunch of J6 Antis. Honest.

Honest? Listen to yourself. Remember Berlin, 1946?

Berlin? 1946? I never been to Berlin.

You were in Berlin two years ago when you ran the mergers and acquisitions team…

I was not, pal. I did not go to Berlin. Where's Berlin?

Lost in history, my son, lost in the history books you didn't read 'cause Major Magat and his Master Magats burned history and now those prog bastards are going to boil us and eat us.

They're gonna boil us and eat us?

Maybe they won't eat us.

Why won't they eat us?

Because we're rotten capitalists and there's no wine that washes rot down.

You sure they got Major Magat?

They got him. In Sinverguenza. With a platoon of his money-men.

Money-men?

The gazillionaires who bought the country.

Those guys. You mean the Technos.

Half a dozen of them.

Did they boil them?

I heard that they shrank him down to size though. I heard that they do that—

Do what?

Shrink 'em. Then they peel 'em then boil their testicles in cauldrons of their own cum.

So they don't castrate us?

You haven't listened to a word I've said in the last four years.

I listened.

All you listened to were your half-assed conspiracy theories and you know it.

You hungry? Maybe we just peel out some of that canned meat for a snack.

Listen to yourself, Mr. Numbnuts. No. Too late. Too much evidence. Can't bury it all. Can't eat it. Can't sell it. Not enough time. Remember Berlin

Berlin. Berlin. Tell me again what happened in Berlin.

December. Year Four of the Culling
Office of Strategic Violence. Committee Room

In the fourth year of the Culling, the war against the Magats has thinned the committee down to four—the General, her aide-de-camp—a tall, Darkskinned woman with tight lips and searing eyes—and two Progs—a Captain and his Lieutenant. Men I have not met but men I read as battle-hardened.

The General has changed since I last saw her in the time before the Culling. Then, she wore the eagle insignia of the colonel. She has risen during this, The Time of Trials and now she wears the sky-blue uniform with three stars on her collar while her aide-de-camp has the colonel's birds on her epaulets and a silver band on her left wrist.

I see that the two Progs—fierce eyes, down-turned mouths—exude the ever-present animal awareness of threat in the defensive way each of them sits back to the wall. These are warriors. Men with the savage look of humans who have bled, who have drawn blood, who have survived the four-year hell of Major Magat's White Christian Nationalist Thanatopian tragedy…and they are armed.

The General looks at me—a quick glance at my hands—then back to the table. Taking my place against the wall beside the warriors I listen to the General—her voice tired, her eyes dark and worried, her now long hair tied back with a black band.

No, Captain, you won't kill him.

We have him trapped in a cul-de-sac, General, with a cadre of Technobillionaires and a squad of MMPPS who're trying to skip with him. We have to go in hard because the MMPPS are killers and butchers and they won't come out except feet first.

Captain, MM has to be skinned alive and if you kill

him, he won't know that pain.

A peelatorium then?

First a castratorium then a peelatorium. A fleshateria....

Fleshateria? I haven't heard it called that before, General.

Magatism has forced us to find new words for terror, Captain. No purity left in Armendrica after the Culling. You know that.

Yes sir, but it seems about right after what he has done to the country.

Yes. To all of us. And the trial will be televised...Still...

Hard truth, General.

Armendricans have to witness his shame...have to know how he betrayed them and why he betrayed them by setting up his delusional Thanatopia and how they betrayed the country with their insular blind acceptance of his horrors.

Shame? General? That kind has no shame. It won't be easy, but I'd take him out, shoot him in the head then burn him and flush his bones down the sewer in Sinverguenza Square.

Not enough, Captain. If I could, I'd capture him, dress him in a cape of the hides he has torn off our people and parade him down Sinverguenza Boulevard at high noon. He has to own the skins. He has to see the cans of meat. The clown has to pay for his genocide, his stupidity, his skein of crimes. No, Captain. It has to end with MM Seashol hanging head down, hooks in his tendons just the way fascist killers must always hang. He betrayed millions, the first term, killed millions the second. He betrayed Armendrica when he aligned with the murderous Bear. He turned our future into a wasteland.

The aide-de-camp wipes at her eyes, head bowed. The silver bracelet sparkles.

Sitting quiet in the quiet room. I watch the Captain and his lieutenant—a bulky man with a shaved head, tufts of black hair on the backs of huge hands. They both are in military dress blues—shiny boots, brass insignia polished to a showcase sheen.

From Day One, it was only ever about himself and the silk-suited men, never about the rest of us.

So, General, if we do it your way, who gets the knife?

The General looks at her aide-de-camp.

Will a survivor fill the bill, Captain?

A survivor?

They took the Colonel on the first night of Day One, Captain. I won't go into the details of her ordeal and I won't ask her to tell you about her escape or to show you the scars. I know you've seen the way the Magats worked in those First Times and here you see a survivor who took the hard way back…Not many came back….

The General's voice turns dark, ripe with anger, bright with an edge of pain.

The Captain and his lieutenant stand. They salute the aide-de-camp.

She takes a deep breath. She pulls a black-handled folding karambit from her pocket. I see that it is eight units from handle to the curved fang tip. The metal glistens in her hand. She says,

For his crimes against women. For his crimes against humanity.

DXM

August 24th Year Four of the Butcher

Today, the golden house is silent as I follow the Colonel—now head of the Office of Strategic Violence—into the palm tree-surrounded mansion. Two warriors flank her as she enters.

The MMPPS, at first resistant, fall silent when the Prog Warriors enter the mansion in full battle gear.

In silence the taking of weapons.

The arrests without bloodshed.

I look at the bowed heads of the MMPPS and have to wonder how many Darkskins this squad murdered after the Clemency on Day One.

Make Armendrica White Again.

The silence of fifty armed burly bearded men in black camo can be explained with one word—Shame. That is the way I will write it. Post it. Send it out. Now that I can work again. Now that the Progs have deposed the Butcher of Armendrica.

In the mansion's silence I hear low-level chanting in the golden room. The same golden room where Major Magat sat in his golden chair the day he sold Armendrica to Lord Skum and Lord Caryan and the Pluts. But the room is not the orderly room of the wealthy with their maids and butlers and cleaning girls who dust and sweep and mop up the messes of the rich. Now, half the room—itself half the size of a gymnasium—is filled with stacks of bibles. Gold covers, thick bibles, all signed by Major Magat and priced with a tag that would embarrass a snake oil salesman. And the boxes of watches—gold watches—stacks of boxes of watches, all still sealed in their little plastic tombs. And stacks and stacks of shoe boxes—piles and mountains of shoe boxes, each one still labeled—signed by Major Magat. Armendrica, Project 2025 Make Armendrica White Again.

Today he is dressed in a uniform that is not Armendrican but a mish-mash military garb—maybe a gift from the Bear to thank him for all his kind words and his efforts to destroy…well…everything. He has ballooned. He bulges out of the uniform. He looks like a little boy who has grown out of his little boy clothes and needs his mama to buy him a new wardrobe. He is huge, but we will shrink him.

Gold. Gold braid on gold epaulets. On his chest, he wears a rainbow of medals and ribbons and combat awards including the Armendrican Medal of Honor (self-bestowed in Year One—the New Year of New Life in Armendrica with Prog chicanery), the Knighthood of the Order of the Pranglian Empire and a plastic copy of the Laurentian Légion d'honneur—often riciculed in the Laurentian press as evidence of a little boy man-child playing at being a soldier.

Mister Major Magat sir?

Major Magat pulls the head off a doll. There are hundreds of dolls…He lines them up and then decapitates them. One at a time. The dolls are Black and Yellow. Red and White. Chanting, he giggles as he rips each body apart and tosses it into a large pile in a corner of the room. The heads he hurls into another. The chant is a rhythm I have heard dozens of times at the rallies, at the speeches, at the Seawenn Conference. He has made a ditty out of the death.

Make—bam
Armendrica—rip
White—bam
Again—rip
Mister Major Magat, sir.

Major Magat looks up. His eyes vacant. His expression malignant obnoxiousness that seethes with self-importance.

He opens a new box of dolls.

Takes them out.

One by one.
Lines them up around the table.
Mister Major Magat, sir, we are here to arrest you.
Red doll—rips the head off. Tosses it away.
Black doll—rips the head off. Tosses it away.
Yellow doll—rips the head off. Tosses it away.
White doll. Fondles the white doll. Strokes the long, blond hair. Touches the legs of the White Doll. Kisses the plastic lips of the White Doll.

I feel invaded. Diminished. Haunted. Once again, the hands on me are the hands and fingers that have invaded women not just of Armendrica but everywhere—in Kleisthenesia, in the Occupied Zones, at the Borders and the Magat-built female public humiliation factories. How many women live feeling that those fingers have peeled their skin down to the bone? Live feeling those penetrating fingers violating them, a feeling that dampens but never goes away.

I hold back the surge in my throat. Feel the fingers again.

Revulsion.

Major Magat waddles to a long gold-plated chest set against a wall. He opens the chest, lays the White Doll in a nest with hundreds of other White Dolls—and I wonder, just wonder why there are no White Boy Dolls in that gold plated chest.

Major Magat glances at the Colonel.
Closes the gold-plated chest.
Returns to the table.
Opens another box of dolls and sets the dolls out.
Red.
Black.
Yellow.
White.
And I wonder—where are the Brown Dolls?
Jesus loves the little children. All the Children of

*the world. Red and Yellow, Black and White, They are
precious in his sight. Jesus loves the little children of the
world.*

Again, revulsion sweeps over me and I am on the
verge of crying as I remember one day, long before
MAWA, I wrote about a little girl who came home from
summer bible camp and said to her mother, Jesus hates me
Mama. No darling, whatever makes you think Jesus hates
you? He hates me because the song we learned today says
he loves all the children of the world—red and yellow
black and white—but he doesn't love brown children and I
am brown, Mama.

*Where are the Brown Dolls, Mister Major Magat,
sir?*

Arrest me? I am Major Magat. I am the World's
Greatest Leader. I am the savior of the white race.

No sir, Mister Major Magat, sir, you are no longer
either of those things.

I am the testicular head of Armendrican everything.
I am the law. I am the living god. I am the deliberavatling
God from the commie prog infestation of Armendrican
honey and unbeadible freedom of choice to die when I
speak the death-words, so just who do you think you are
doing what to? Assnode?

Yes sir, yes to all of that, sir, and you are Major
Magat, sir and we are arresting you and you are going on
trial for the crime of eating people.

People? Blackskins aren't people so it's no more a
crime than eating dog is a crime.

So, Mister Major Magat, sir, you admit that you ate
people meat?

Did I say that? I don't remember saying that. It's
fake news. All lies. All that prog socialist anti-armendrican
bog snoggy is fake and there are alternative facts to support
my truth telling all the way down the line shall we dance?

That's opinion, Mister Major Magat, sir. An

alternative truth as you have said many times, but we have
evidence that you ordered the extermination of all
Darkskinned people, and as you can see, Mister Major
Magat, sir, I am a Darkskinned person and I am still here.
In addition to the charges of eating human meat, Mister
Major Magat, sir, there are other counts against you
including Congenital Zaniism and the Naked Butchering of
the nation of Armendrica. And so, Mister Major Magat, sir,
I am arresting you.

You little poison-pricksack. You brown-hided
vermin. What have you poisoned today? The air? The
water? The blood of White Armendricans? I will hunt you
down and burn your passport get the hell out of my country
because we're coming and we will hunt you down and eat
your libtard leftie prog commie ass.

Armendrica is no longer 'your country,' Mister
Major Magat, sir, so this Darkskinned woman will change
your diaper and then we will lead you to jail where you will
have Bannonmagat the WeepMasterMagat and Herr
Meister Fascist Magat Flint to sing your praises and to keep
you company during your dark night of the slammer.

You can't arrest me. The MJ's made sure of that,
crawl back into your libtard tent.

You are under arrest, Mister Major Magat Seashol,
for butchery and for sending twenty-six million people to
their death by cause of your policies. Sir. So please. Hands
behind your back.

But my hair.

Your hair under that helmet, Mister Major Magat,
sir, looks like a shredded carrot.

Oh stop with the flattery, you slimy little brown
vermin with your slimy brown pussy who never voted for
me.

The Colonel shackles Major Magat. The steel cuffs
cut into the pudgy hand with its tiny fingers, fingers that
with a wiggled scrawl, in other times, sent thousands of us

to die—in the camps, in the tent cities, at the borders, in the peelatoria....

And I remember Timothy who wrote, before the Retribution Act of Year 3, that a nation never fully recovers from the yoke of a fascist regime built on hate, deadlock, demonization of internal and external enemies, and complicity by existing elites. The Pluts. That existing Armendrican elite who have forgotten who made them rich.

Flicker—TV cameras. Teams of reporters. Hundreds of video setups. A circus tent inside the courtroom.

Flicker—A very skinny Major Magat—in prison grays that appear to be three sizes too large for him— stands with a dozen Minor and Master Magats, Captos and Pluts all wearing headphones and chained to a bank of benches. At a podium, a ProgLawyer reads indictments from a parchment scroll six fingers thick....

Count 125—Betrayal of the Armendrican Constitution
Count 126—Distilling the underclass to bio-fuel
Count 127—Treason
Count 128—Butchery
Count 129—Genocide
Count 130—Torture of dissidents
Count 131—Unlawful imprisonment
Count 132—Willful and illegal non-compliance with Laws
Count 133—Child abuse and incestuous congress
Count 134—

Flicker—In a castratorium major magat seashol chained naked to a rack. A soldier, a woman, in dress blues and holding a karambit, slices the seashol genitals releasing a spurt of blood. And then, she inserts the tip of the karambit in the gash and peels the flesh from the body of the bleeding once-upon-a-time-has been dictator.

Flicker—Lord Skum hanging from hooks in his Achilles tendons, his skin a sack around his neck. On his checkbook on the floor—Balance Zero.

Flicker—Lord Caryan gutted and hanging from hooks, lowered into a cauldron of boiling water.

YOU

You enter the roaster. The heat sears the skin of your face, your hands. You feel the heat burrow through your shirt. The heat is not pleasant.

You see that the building is a long row of roasters and on the roasters you see bodies—turning brown in the heat of the flames and their fat flares into flumes of smoke and the smoke smells...like...You're not sure—it's a smell you do not know but it is pungent, scorched.

You hear the sizzle of fat in the flame of each roaster as you walk the line and at the end of the line, you see Darkskinned men and Darkskinned women dressed in loin clothes and sleeveless shirts. They are black of hair and thin and trim—athletes muscular and of good size. You ask a woman—one of the Darkskinned women with black hair—

What do you do with the...

Bodies?

Yes. The roasted bodies.

You think we eat them?

No. Yes. Well. I hope not.

We're browning them. Put a little color on them.

What then?

When they come out of the roasters…

You bury them?

There are wolves and hyenas waiting...

This isn't...

What you expected of us? What did you expect of us?

Not revenge. Not on this scale.

Revenge?

The woman, standing at the last roaster, touches your arm. She smiles. You see white teeth. A mouth with lips as arched as any bow, eyes the color of pink coral. You have never seen eyes that pink, that pure, that true and You know the truth now.

Are you?

Yes, she says. I am.

How many?

How many of us?

That too, but those. The others.

Those that didn't escape into Lord Skum's astral dream when he gave up on Terra...those we caught in the first sweep. Those who wanted to put us back in their capitalist chains...those who...financed the destruction and the collapse of laws, the laws that kept US in chains. There are always consequences to greed and privilege...and their dream after the Culling was that they could buy us and that we would forgive them and let them once again forge the chains but....

Wait. Wait...You're telling me...

Something you didn't know?

Something I wish I had known.

If there is no law then anything is possible.

Possible? Including this...this...

This balancing act surprises you.

Surprise? A little. More than a little.

What did you think would happen when they killed curiosity?

A little...acceptance...would...do...

Oh no. NO. NO and NO again. We sat outside too long.

And now?

They stole every pound of meat, every ounce of fat from our bodies in the Times of Crisis and Culling. They said they would build a new world, but all they did was change the chains and the locks and they built their palaces again and they...

There she stopped. You look at her. She does not sob. She does not cry. She does not apologize. The coral pink eyes do not blink. Her gaze has force and depth and she peers into You and You feel her reborn power and that power is nothing You have seen or felt or heard of— renewed from the inside out and transformed and changed into a different human being.

What now?

What now? Soon we will have cleared Armendrica of them and their seed will live only in the guts of hyenas and we will build the first world that is not built on their crimes against us. You will see it...

A shining mansion on a hill?

No mansions. No palaces. No privilege.

No humans?

You still don't see? You still don't realize what they did and why they did it and how they did it. You choose not to see?

But the killing?

You think of justice but you don't see the truth that justice comes with freedom and for...thousands of years the genius of Armendrica was locked away in the genes of peasants who had their flesh whipped from them, who had their women raped and butchered, who had their children starved and enslaved and kept in ignorance. That's the truth but now...this is a new country and this country is ours— the once poor, the once butchered have taken control.

She leaves You. She turns to the roasters and the meat and the fat sizzling into the roasters and You see sweat beautiful and slick and shiny coating her body and You walk past the roasters, past death and for the first time You do not shudder nor do you hesitate.

You knew it had come to this—

Based on Actual and/or Probable Events
some of which may or may not have already occurred.

Glossary & Acronyms

AMM2—After Major Magat 2—the current and reprehensible fascist, hate-mongering and murderous epoch following the second election of Major Magat and the dissolution of all foreign trade. AKA the *Culling*.

BMM1—Before Major Magat 1— the social, cultural, and educational establishment Before MM's first and catastrophic administration. Often seen as Halcyon Days when, despite the murderous practice of killing, the Magats had not yet declared education illegal, a decree (or EO) which led to the death of curiosity.

Capto—Capitalist—the bringers of ruination and deterioration to Armendrican economics as the already vulture-capitalism degenerated into hedgefundism and Technoauthoritarianism, which led to the demise of Armendrican industry and the designation of Armendrica to a failed-state in MM's isolationist world.

Castratorium—*Plural-castratoria.* Any high school gymnasium, abandoned hospital, abandoned warehouse, or industrial-slaughter site where Magats worked their *gonadal resectioning.* Related to the *peelatorium.*

CMJ—Chief Magat Justice—the Head Magat Justice. The first of Nine, also known as a gutless, spineless, mealy-mouthed mouther of platitudes and evasionist, isolationist, lop-sided diction. Refers to everyone below his/her/their rank as *they.*

Culling—Another term for Genocide. When Major Magat declared war on the Immies, the reflex from the Minor Magats was *to thin the herd.* In Magat-speak, the Herd was any of the non-White, non-Christian peoples living in Armendrica. Note the close relationship between killing and culling. In the bubble-mind of the Minor Magats, there is no difference between killing steers and culling the Brownskins and Blackskins.

Dexter—Right Wing Magat Fanatic. Incapable of seeing or understanding the inherent contradictions of Magatism. Also a low-information voter uprooted and dismayed at their self-annihilation when they discover that in voting Magatistic, they voted against their own interests. This knowledge doesn't in any way cancel their hatred of the Libs…whom they think they own.

Dhaler—the basic unit of money in Armendrica. One hundred kentz equal one dhaler. A currency no longer accepted in the world market as the worthless treasure of a Failed State.

DXM—Déesse ex machina. The Female Voice and Mind of the Omnipresent Narrator. This is the Conscience of a Nation speaking through the Female. In *Armendrica*, there is no Protagonist. The DXM and the OPN are the choral voices that remain silent in the various forms of Magat but which speak clearly to the Progs, Libtards, and Lefties. It is possible that the DXM and OPN are the Evolved Voices of Education speaking through time. DXM and OPN are the ghosts of banished journalists practicing their craft in the thin air of truth left in Armendrica. Hunted as animals by Magats.

ELPs—Exiled Libtards and/or Progs. The MMPPS hunt down and persecute the pols Major Magat Seashol blackballed as being disloyal to Magatism and therefor unworthy of being left alive. In the first Culling, Magats drove Progs into exile and sent killers to quiet them when they spoke out.

GLP—Greedy Little Puke—A puppet nurtured on alternative facts, truth social indoctrination, Vulpine news sources. Deeply racist and misogynist. Often called an **incel**.

Immie—Magat shorthand for immigrant. Immies are the enemy. Easy to spot. Easy to kill. No distinction between country of origin so all Immies are lumped into the Brownskin category. Most Immies hold menial jobs that the Minor Magats refuse because it's not work for a White Man. In the dog-whistle-mantra-speak of Magats, immies are stealing jobs that belong to White Men. The contradiction is lost on the Magats as they are swamped with the politics of resentment and divisiveness.

Incel—Involuntary celibate. Incels are GLPs who can't form attachments with women either because they are ugly, malnourished, ignorant, or stupid. GLPs are inveterate wankers who beat their meat while watching Bear Porn and guzzling hi-energy sugar-free beverages.

KE—Kukulkanian Emissary. Emissary educated in diplomacy with degrees from universities in Laurentia, Kleisthenesia, and Prerugginia. Post-doctoral research in Armendrica. Fluent in six languages including Laurentian, Kleisthenesian, Preruggian, and Armendrican. Author of numerous works on Armendrican politics including deep studies of Armendrican educational systems BMM1 and AMM2. One time Kukulkanian ambassador to OBUP. She declined the position of Secretary-General after MM withdrew support from OBUP.

Kleisthenesia—The birthplace of democracy now a puppet state fed by the mendacious, meretricious pseudo-dictator.

KP—Kukulkanian president not a fan of insurgent Armendricans who, as refugees, have no bargaining power, but still make demands on the Kukulkanians for ammo, food to replace the meat Ready to Eat, and first class accommodations in the tent cities on the Southern Border.

Kukulkania—The Southernmost neighbor of Armendrica. Often characterized by Magats as the source of all that's evil and immigrant, a position that's at odds with the

Magat-Armendrican reliance on immigrant labor.

Laurentia—The Northernmost neighbor of Armendrica.

Lord Skum—The immigrant traitor who bought Major Magat and turned Armendrica into an empty shell as he touted the Plutocracy as a model for the ages. Lord Skum now qualifies as that most MAGAT brand of pseudo-Christian—a hypocrite who exploited religion to amplify his own power and wealth—with a heavenly license to bully the weak. His coup d'état ruined the lives of people and seems much more like the devil's work. He is arrested, tried, sentenced, and deported.

Magatism—a conglomeration of White Post-Christian religion, nationalism, capitalism, and crippled republicanism. Magatism can be characterized as the absolute nadir of human existence with its emphasis of death, destruction, isolationism, predatory hedgefundism and post-dated resurrection. Centered on the Cult of Major Magat, Magatism is history re-written history corrupted education corrupted and outlawed except for the home-schooled crippled system, corrupted and plundered legal system and destroyed democratic politics by building Zaniism into every node of Armendrican life.

Major Magat—the highest ranking Magat. Former First Magat but after J6 commonly known as a liar, rapist, welsher, traitor. Also known as a chiseler, defrauder, grifter, scammer, swindler, and narcissist. Often portrayed as a god, or sometimes a fat clown. Also known as the "testicular head" of Armendrican fascism.

Metaphor—a figure of speech in which a word or phrase is applied to an object or action to which it is not literally applicable. Every word in *Armendrica* is metaphor from Culling to Cannibalism. No word is *literally* applicable, but the Reader knows instinctively how to read *Armendrica* at the archetypal level and associate the archetypes to the times. **Archetype**—a form which the instincts assume but are realized only when brought into Place and Time.

MM—Master Magat—a sycophantic, ass-kissing lieutenant. A True Believer in Magatism. One responsible for carrying out Major Magat's wishes, expressed or implied. A high-level criminal. A facilitator who finds ways to inject fake truth into MM's lies. Also known as an apologist, planner, and dirty trickster who will lie, cheat, and kill for MM then find ways to pass the buck to Libtards and Progs. Present at the Seawenn Conference.

MM—Minor Magat—A brain-damaged acolyte who follows any Master Magat's orders regardless of the stupidity or ignorance of the order. Sometimes follows un-written and/or unspoken orders which allows for Zero accountability on the Master Magat's part. Because all MMs sound alike, there is no way to differentiate individuals hence the double M designation in all interactions. This leads to levels of confusion which are useful in denial.

MMPPS—Major Magat Personal Protection Squads—Extermination squads modeled on the historic Schutzstaffel or SS. Major Magat swore the MMPPS to a single purpose—to hunt down and murder any Armendrican who opposed, voted against, or satirized Major Magat during either of his campaigns to install himself as king and to destroy democracy in Armendrica.

MJ—Magat Justice—one of nine on the Upper Court (often jokingly referred to as the Supper Court). MJs are Indistinguishable one from the other, as they were all appointed by Seashol at the last cleansing so they are known only by their number, e.g. Magat Justice 1, 2, 3…

MW—Magat Wife—The Magat Wife is the perfect mate for the Master Magat and the Minor Magat. They have trained her to ask no questions, to home-school the children, to restrict her movements to the kitchen, the bedroom, and the church. She is best when she gives silent approval to the Master Magat's genocidal tendencies while guarding her own offspring from the horror of a Prog world and its Socialist framers—the Authors of the Constitution.

Magatte—A rare specimen often educated, and adept at what she does, but paradoxically born without a conscience, moral sense or sense of logic which allows her to ignore facts, science, history, all the while accepting as absolute truth every word that oozes from Major Magat's mouth. Sometimes conflated with the Karens as a Hater. One who fails to see that there are consequences to hate-speech and hate-action.

Mencius Moldbug—founder of Dark Enlightenment. Often spoken of as a mythical character whose influence on Major Magat exists only in the minds of other Technoautocratic thinkers. Dark Enlightenment is characterized by its anti-democratic and anti-egalitarian views, advocating for a return to hierarchical and authoritarian forms of governance and sometime/onetime purveyor of bio-fuel distilled from the bodies of the hapless lower classes.

OBUP—The Operational Bureau of Unspent-national funds in the Public Interest.

OPN—Omnipresent Narrator—OPN is the voice and mind of the writer—not the author. *Armendrica* has no Protagonist which makes it a bit of a struggle for the reader. But…Stick with it…the reward is a new way to look at fiction and it will make you ask yourself why the SMOF (Standard Model of Fiction) has persisted in the writing world.

OPN and DXM—banned journalists struggling to stay anonymous because MM has declared war on them and banned all sources of "fake news." They have good sources but nowhere to post their writing because MM and Lord Skum have cancelled the internet except for "official outlets" which only LS and MM can use. This leaves OPN and DXM with the darkweb for their writing—chances are that LS and MM know that it exists but in their limited and negative world they don't know now to access it.

Peelatorium—Plural *peelatoria*—Any available site in the meat-packing or slaughterhouse districts where the Magats perfected their *epidermal cleansing* techniques.

Plut—Plutocrat—a Magat who claims to be a self-made man but was born in the normal, biological manner from a woman's uterus. Though the beneficiary of a trust fund built by and bequeathed from immigrant parents, the plutocrat still claims to be self-made and is fiercely anti-immigrant unless the immigrant is also self-made. Avid supporter of both the peelatoria and castratoria even though the *epidermal cleansing* resulted in catastrophic shortages of workers—the underclass.

Prerugginia—One-time—pre-MM 1—trading partner with Armendrica but now relegated to Occupied Zone status worthy only of receiving tainted goods. Prime customer for Meat Ready to Eat and leather products from the peelatoria.

ProgPhar—Progressive Pharmacist—Progressive *fill in the profession* or any educated, competent professional who saw the MI (Magat Insanity) for what it is—fascistic, idol worship but still determined to provide the best service possible for any survivors of the DEI cleansing the Magats initiated.

ROM—Really Old Magat—Really Old Magats are sexagenarians, septuagenarians, and octogenarians who backed Major Magat and their policies. AKA as Armendricans who voted against their own self-interest then wonder what the hell happened to their safety net and medical coverage. Often depicted as shaven-headed, toothless and decrepit elders who reek of urine because the Lord Skum's Network outlawed leakage pads.

Seashol—Anagrammatic cognomen of Major Magat. (adjective/noun/metaphor)

Technos—Technoauthoritarians—the subclass of billionaires who, as early digital entrepreneurs and visionaries, raised hopes of a coded future, but then relapsed into overlordism. Those responsible for crushing the underclass of "worthless" parasites and distilling them into biofuel. Their goal is to find an acceptable alternative to genocide.

Teutonknia—A former fascist dictatorship that murdered twenty million people and became the model for P2025 the treasonous program for voiding the Armendrican Constitution. P 2025 includes Aktion T 4 as a solution to the progress of science.

Thanatopia—The death-world of the Xters. From *Thanatos, the personification of death.* The Magats didn't know it, but their theocratic experiment failed on Day One with the first Cull. Thanatopia—the Magat-created death-world on the only blue spot in the cosmos.

Timothy—Timothy Snyder. Author. *On Tyranny*—Twenty Lessons from the Twentieth Century. The standard text now required reading in public schools following the Restoration.

Xter—White Christian Nationalist (pronounced kryster…)—often described as a brain-dead, low information Magatist voter with no compunctions with outlawing all other religions. While stealing the name Christian, the Xter has disavowed the moral and ethical lessons of the Judean master and allows the money-lenders into the temple.

You—You, the reader. You are in this record. You—

woman, man, girl, boy—have felt the fear and the dread, have seen the blood and terror, smelled the rot of Major Magat and Lord Skum as they rape the city, the country, the nation and spin their Thanatopian misery across the bodies of the dead. You have witnessed the cataclysm, seen the destruction every day. You, reader, are now a part of the horror that will infect your grandchildren with a disease for which is no vaccine. That is the future…

Zani—One of many anagrams the AUR (Armendrican Underground and Resistance) developed beginning with MM1 and ending with the Restoration and Major Magat Seashol's imprisonment and delayed shrinking and flaying for treason.

Woman—A quasi-human being in the Magat mindset often used for pussy-grabbing and for perverse sexual practices, but mainly for pussy-grabbing and cooking. Always last in any sequential arrangement.

About The Author

Jay Laurent Merick is a pseudonym. His whereabouts are unknown. We know little about his life or his writing. Although he states that he has written twenty-four books, there is no evidence that this is a fact. It is entirely possible that he doesn't exist but is the figment of the editor's fragmented mind—which would make him a fictional creature posing as a legitimate author.